THE GOLDEN PIN

Annette Carolyn Ely

Dear Barb,
I love you dearly,
Thank you for helping
make life beautiful
for me,
Love,
Annette
Carolyn
Ely.

MINERVA PRESS
LONDON
ATLANTA MONTREUX SYDNEY

THE GOLDEN PIN
Copyright © Annette Carolyn Ely 1998

All Rights Reserved

ISBN 1 86106 695 3

First Published 1998 by
MINERVA PRESS
195 Knightsbridge
London SW7 1RE

Printed in Great Britain for Minerva Press

Chapter One

Pamela dreamily caressed the champagne lace across the knee of her peignoir with her tiny forefinger. The half-moon of her buffed, naturally pink fingernail looked pretty against the champagne snowflake which had been created by some patient woman's expertise with a crochet hook.

"It's wonderful that Mr. Randolph relished the idea of sending me to Minnesota for a few weeks leave," she smiled to herself thinking that it would be a perfect solution for the dilemma at the Arizona architectural firm where she presently worked. Contemplating the sudden recession in which Randolph Architectural and Design had suddenly found itself, Pamela remembered Mr. Randolph's naturally kind face clouded by concern for his associates when he had been forced to announce a cut-back in personnel the day before.

"I find that in order to keep our projects moving at all, we must temporarily lay a few people off. In order to keep those of you who will be getting this unexpected vacation afloat, I have suggested to the Board of Directors that your mutually owned company funds be made available to you for loans, at a minimum interest rate thereby providing you with adequate income until such time as we can reconvene operations on a full scale. That, together with your workman's compensation, should get you through the next two months without eating into your own personal savings and investments. I am open to suggestion, if any of you have ideas which could improve upon mine. But, be sure that you will be called back to work full time in two months and then we will all sink or swim together." Phoenix, Arizona shimmered in the sunlight through the window behind his salt and peppery head.

Pamela couldn't help but admire Mr. Randolph's candor. An architect of renown, the recipient of numerous awards for excellence in design and quality building, he had retained his elegant, yet unpretentious manner. She was proud to be his protégé. Having started as his secretary and finding friendship coupled with the joy of working for a truly exceptional boss who didn't mind kicking off his Florsheims in order to sit cross-legged on the floor with her as they pored over columnar pads the size of her desk top, she relished going to work every morning. It was during one of these relaxed sessions that she had first seen a worried look come across Mr. Randolph's handsome face.

"Pamela, I don't like what I see here. It doesn't look good," he slowly raised a brown, earthen mug to his lips and softly sipped coffee. Lowering the cup, he looked over at her. In a characteristic, impetuous burst of optimism, he grinned at her.

"How would you like to take a few weeks off at my expense and take that tow-headed boy of yours up to his grandpa and grandma's farm in northern Minnesota for a bit of fishing?"

"Oh, Mr. Randolph. Do you truly mean that? But, what will you do without me?"

"Oh," he answered with a wry smile, "although I will miss you and your charming way of flustering all my colleagues when they first walk through the office door, I think I'll be able to answer the telephone and hold them at bay until you get back. Of course, I can't make coffee worth a tinker, but maybe with a little practice I'll get the hang of it."

Affecting a pout, Pamela retorted playfully, "Are you suggesting that all I am good for around here is adding color and flavor?"

Mr. Randolph laughed and started closing the columnar pad carefully. "You know better than that, my dear. You have become my right hand and if I weren't planning to take a two week break myself during the next month and then extend it into a buying trip to Europe, I wouldn't let you out of my sight. I value your impeccable taste too greatly. As a matter of fact, I want to take you along to scour the English countryside in a search for artefacts and antiques with which to decorate our current project, the Anglican Club. But, after listening to concern for your nine year old as to what he will do during the summer months while school is not in session, I thought that perhaps you would rather have two or three months of paid vacation in order to take him from the streets of Phoenix to the rolling meadows and blue lakes of your native Minnesota. Does that appeal to you?" His eyes twinkled at her over the rim of his ever-present mug of coffee.

How she loved that man! Such a father he had been to her since finding herself widowed; and in him she had found solace in looking for a meaningful career. She had been impressed by this honorable man who had been touched by her efforts to keep her problems to herself, not to mention her exceptional skills.

"Oh, Mr. Randolph. Do you really mean that? But, how can you afford it with the company in a slump?"

"Don't worry about how I can afford it," he smiled. "Whether I take you along with me to Europe and slave-drive you there, or send you north with your cub for three months will cost approximately the same. So, you see, I intend to do one or the other, but the choice remains yours. I don't want you to feel pressured into accepting the option which constitutes working for the company. I would rather you fill the needs of your fatherless child at this time, not to mention your own. Every boy needs a male image after whom he can model himself to some extent. He needs his uncles and grandfather, don't you think?"

In tears of gratitude which sparkled in addition to the beautiful even smile that had dazzled him the first time he ever laid eyes on her, she looked into his brown optics and whispered, "Thank you." Struggling to keep her composure she bowed her head, thick chestnut colored curls falling forward over her delicate shoulders. A shaft of sunlight streaming through the plate-glass window across the room caught her in its glow and the burnished copper in her hair glinted in the sun, fusing into the golden highlights and deep mysterious browns which graced her fair head.

'What is it that is so touching about that girl?' the elderly Mr. Randolph quietly mused as he watched her. 'I want to reach out and comfort her, protect her as if I were her father... and I will. She's talented, artistic, exceptionally intelligent and smart with that intelligence, works a little too hard if I don't keep tabs on her and is too good looking for her own good...' he mused as he remembered a few incidents which had frightened her during the past few months.

Looking up, Pamela asked, "Would you like another cup of coffee laced with sugar and cream, Randolph style?" She made a wry face at the thought of sweet coffee, which made him laugh.

"No, that's O.K. It's about time to take a jaunt down to the building site to see how far Dick and his fellows have gotten today. I promised that I would make an appearance by three o'clock and I have exactly eight minutes in which to do so."

Pamela rose from the textured carpet, gathering the columnar pad into her arms from which a sterling silver charm bracelet tinkled, making sounds similar to that of miniature ice cubes moving in a stemmed glass of water. The sound was pleasing in the stillness of the smart office, making the creams and deep chocolates of the chairs, couch and pillows, seem even more rich. The eggshell feathers of palomino grass stirred gracefully in a four foot vase beside the couch as the ensemble caught the air coming from the cooler overhead.

"Why don't you go home early tonight and do something out of the ordinary for a change, Pamela? There's nothing pressing around here anymore for today," Mr. Randolph concluded.

"Really? Wonderful! No sooner said then done, Sir!" she exclaimed.

"And, while you are swimming or whatever, why don't you start planning what to take on whichever of the offers you have just received? D-Day is one week from today. And, then it is three months off for you, part of which can be spent with me in Europe, or all of which can be spent with your son in Minnesota. Think it over and let me know on Monday. Suit yourself, O.K.?"

"What a fabulous choice. Oh, Mr. Randolph, you are absolutely the dearest employer a person could ever have!"

"Don't tell the construction crew that," Mr. Randolph chuckled, "I wouldn't want them hugging me too. Now, harness that exuberance and get out of here before I change my mind and make you type up that report on my desk. Scoot!"

Hurriedly tidying her desk, unplugging the coffee pot and grabbing her purse as she walked past the counter, she snapped off the light as Mr. Randolph swept past her out the door. Closing the door firmly, she tried it again to make sure it was locked and walked off with a lilting step which kept time with the joy in her heart. Waving goodbye to Mr. Randolph as he left in his yellow Cadillac, she got into her humble Pinto and thrilled to the tiny engine as it surged forward toward the exit onto 40th Street.

'How did I ever get so lucky as to be employed by him?' she happily thought to herself. 'Brother, what a choice he has given me. Hmmm, there is *no* way I can say no to the needs of my son... but, just maybe I can go to both places – Europe *and* Minnesota. Maybe Davie will want to go to camp!' So thinking, she pulled away from the intersection, zooming through the green light towards home in Paradise Valley.

"Oh, Dear God, how I love those mountains you have made!" she breathed aloud as she drove towards the foothills through the arid desert floor, cacti and sage brush abounding on left and right of the road. Springtime in the desert was a joy, no matter which way one looked at it and she had always marveled at the tiny, exquisite blooms which pushed their delicate yet strong way through the hard-packed desert floor. Some of them were tinier than her smallest fingernail and stood nodding their little colorful heads in the sun as if boasting of their fragile strength. 'I can't even dig this stuff with a spade, how can these tiny stems push through the hard clay and sand?' she had mused during her walks in the desert. She also loved listening to the roadrunners busily gathering tidbits for their young as they scurried between saguaro and barrel cacti, under sage plants and over sticky sand devils in their bare feet.

Later, thinking back on these things, Pamela was unaware that she was smiling as she relaxed in her negligee, having just finished packing swimming gear, jeans and boots for both herself and son. He finally had conquered his excitement and was fast asleep in the adjoining bedroom. She, deliciously tired, was sitting in front of the fireplace in the bedroom, appreciating the warmth against the chill of an unexpected rain that evening. The glow of the flames licked through the redness of the DuBonnet in her goblet as she held it in front of her eyes to enjoy the play of ruby red fire against cut crystal prisms.

'Life, you are interesting, to say the least,' she thought.

The sound of a high-powered engine, softly humming into the drive caught her attention. "Oh no," she sighed. "I hope it is not Mr. DeSilva again! Jill isn't here and he absolutely makes me uncomfortable when she is gone! He's so pompous with his stilted language and airs."

Pamela untucked her bare feet from under her, placing them on the white carpet. Setting her glass on the end table, she quietly rose to go change into something less provocative. Ned DeSilva was a sensuous man and she remembered the passes which he had made toward her during the months he had been courting her best friend, Jill Farthing, with whom she and Davie shared an apartment. Walking into the dressing room, she hastily grabbed a pair of jeans and tunic top. Just as she started unfastening the hook and eye which held her peignoir in place at the bosom, two arms encircled her from behind. She gasped, recognizing Ned's tan muscular arms. Simultaneously, lips brushed hotly against her neck behind her right ear and his hands moved up to claim her breasts. Struggling to free herself first from the hands, she pushed and pulled her head away.

"Ned! let me go!"

"Ah, my darling. Don't fight me," he breathed heavily.

"I said let go!" and she wrenched herself free from his clinging arms. "What would Jill say if she came home right now? You ought to be ashamed of yourself, Ned! After all, you are her fiancé and have no business even teasing like this!"

He crossed his arms over his chest, jewelry glinting in the soft light of the dressing room.

"Why do you always insist that I am merely teasing?" he asked.

"What else could an honorable man be doing since he is engaged to my dearest friend?" she shot an angry look at him.

"He could be trying to get you to believe him when he repeatedly tells you that he made a mistake and wants his fiancée's friend instead – she whom he met only days after his unfortunate proposal of marriage to the wrong one. But no, even though you lay at death's door recuperating from a car accident, you resisted such an idea. Even though I have asked you to do the honorable thing by going with me to tell her that I made a mistake, and that it is you whom I love, you refuse to do so. Your refusal does not change the passionate love I feel for you, Pamela."

"But, it is a love which is not shared in my heart, Ned. I keep telling you so and you refuse to listen to me."

"I refuse to listen to you because you are not telling me the truth. You are speaking out of loyalty to your friend. You do not want to hurt her. But, I refuse to believe that you do not feel as I," his teeth sparkled beneath his dark mustache as he eloquently persuaded with silver tongue.

Feeling somewhat shaken by feelings she didn't understand, Pamela brushed past him, sweeping out into the hall, down to the living room. She came to a standstill beside her mahogany piano. It seemed to lend strength by virtue of having been a gift from her late husband. She needed strength at this moment, for she had never run into animal lust prior to meeting DeSilva, and she didn't recognize its pull, masked as it was in seemingly, a gentleman.

Turning around to face Ned whom she felt standing behind her, Pamela demanded quietly, "How did you get into the house?"

"With the key Jill has given me," Ned smiled. He was nervous, uptight from his repressed desire for Pamela. Pacing the parquet floor like a caged lion, he concentrated on the desire steaming in his loins, trying to calm the tempestuous reaction which feeling her pressed into his arms had given him.

Ned wasn't used to being denied what he wanted. Spoiled by riches all his life, he had experienced only gratification of every desire down to the smallest whim.

'How can she not find me attractive?' his inflated ego made him muse silently. 'She must be lying. There's not a woman in the world who wouldn't find me desirable with my money and my good looks – ah! She must be pretending.'

He recognized good breeding in Pamela. And to match the loveliness was the inherent innocence of the sheltering her parents and deceased husband had lavished to secure her world. Because they were good and without vice, she assumed that the rest of the world was the same.

'Well, my little pet, I can sweep you off your feet for a few fun and games. You are stupid when it comes to men,' so thinking he stopped pacing the floor and looked energetically at her, smiling.

Pamela was the first woman who had ever resisted his charm and obvious wealth. That in itself piqued his interest in her to the point where he could scarcely contain himself in his pursuit of her.

But, Pamela was of loyal stuff made. Betraying a friend was not to her liking and she would not even consider anything so preposterous as this unlikely romance. Attracted to his animal prowess and wealth she was, but it felt wrong to her. It made her feel somewhat ill inside, and being one who followed her instincts when it came to people, she knew to leave untouched this man whom her dearest friend adored,

"Well, even though you have a key to our home, I would appreciate it if you would be gentleman enough in the future to kindly ring the doorbell when it is obvious that Davie and I are at home," she softly demanded with pent up fury. Her grey eyes flashed with anger, belying her soft voice.

"If you insist, Madam," he rejoined, bowing slightly from the waist, ever the Bourgeoisie puppet.

"I insist," she whispered, as something clattered onto the parquet floor, glistening in the soft light from the ruby lampshade.

Stepping swiftly to her side, Ned bent down, "Ah, Madam, allow me to once again present my humble gift, born of admiration for you, which I first sent over with Jill as you lay in the hospital," and he held his hand out to her while taking hers in his other. Pressing something long and slender into her palm, he stood very close.

She could smell the expensive cologne which he was wearing and his closeness and touch made her almost lose her resolve. For a man he was and she had not been near anyone since her husband's death two years earlier. She grasped the edge of the piano with her left hand.

'But, it feels wrong,' she struggled within herself, 'it is all wrong. Something is missing, I truly don't care for this man!' Looking down she saw the golden pin, fashioned of eighteen carat gold, graced with the coolness of an emerald set in its head, lying in her hand. She remembered the gift, so welcome when she was in the hospital, for at that time things had not been complicated. He was merely Jill's friend and a new brother figure for herself. He had given Jill one exactly like it and initialed both with the proper letters. He had said it was because they were obviously near twins in spirit that he wanted to give them like gifts.

Contemplating these things, she thought of giving it back to him on the spot, but thought better of it when remembering Jill's delight that similar hair pins would grace her blond hair while adorning that of Pamela's dark curls. Pamela looked into Ned's face with a level, cool gaze, and murmured, "Thank you." Raising her arms to reinsert the adornment into her hair, she felt a surge of relief pass through her at the sound of Jill's Porsche winding up to the house. Light footsteps crunched across the gravelly sand between the Mexican tiles that made up the walk, emitting an occasional hollow click of a high heel as it struck a tile. Pamela went to the sturdy oaken door to open it for her friend.

Looking into the unsuspecting sweet countenance of her dearest friend, Pamela felt like crying. She involuntarily threw her arms around Jill's neck. The pressure Ned had been applying suddenly seemed overwhelming.

"I'm so glad to see you," she exclaimed. "Come on, I have a surprise for you in the living room."

"Could that surprise be a certain gentleman whose golden pins we wear in our hair?" Jill smiled, "His car is in the parking lot."

"You are too smart for your own good!" Pamela sighed. "Come on and tame the wild beast in your man." And she tucked her arm into Jill's as they headed toward the parlor.

"Ah, my dear!" Ned swept Jill into his arms and kissed her gently on both cheeks. Taking her exquisite face between his hands, he kissed the tip of her nose and then offered to take the books and packages from her arms,

"How were classes this evening, my lovely?"

Glowing like an enamored schoolgirl, Jill responded, "Just fine."

Pamela watched as Ned's silken manner completely swamped Jill with adoring feelings of being the only one in his world... the only woman he possibly could care for. Feeling disgusted at the cunning of the man and at his lack of conscience which made him so deceptive, she turned aside so as not to witness the pure love of her friend being adulterated by the complete worldliness of such pretense.

Yet, as she watched, she remembered him saying, "I love you more, but I also love Jill, and if I can't have you, I will have Jill. I will have *one* of you." And because of her lack of exposure to polygamous men, she felt confused.

So remembering this, she retired to her bedroom, where she carefully locked the door, then sat upon the white velvet coverlet, contemplating the ways of men, of love, of life.

Life. Life. What was it all about, when the one you adored was snatched prematurely away from his wife and child, when accidents befell? And, yet, 'Life is beautiful with all its intrigue, its many faceted people, its beauties of nature. I opt for living this life to the fullest,' Pamela thought as she undressed her hair, lying the golden pin carefully on the mirrored organizer of her dressing table.

'Ah, Mr. Randolph. I have made up my mind to accept both of your proposals, providing Davie decides to go to Boys Camp for two weeks in August. But, I am not going to force him into a decision. I will let him choose, knowing that if he goes there, I will be flying to Europe for a buying trip. We'll meet in Minneapolis upon our return if that is what Davie chooses. In the meantime, I relish the idea of escaping to Minnesota, away from Ned's clandestine overtures, which I sincerely despise. Besides, I embrace the chance to recover from the accident.'

Snapping the bedside lamp off, Pamela nestled between the percale sheets, feeling the stiff eyelet trim rubbing against her chin as she buried herself deeper into the pillows. She could hear the soft murmur of Ned and Jill's animated conversation and occasional laughter down the hall, and the soft steady breathing of her nine year old whose bedroom was next to hers.

Feeling a surge of love for the little miniature of her departed husband, whose movements were brought to her via the monitor on the nightstand, she fell into an untroubled sleep; savoring the fact that after one more day of work at the office, she and her little one would climb aboard Flight 426, leaving all their worries behind for three wonderful months.

'How lucky can I be?' she smiled to herself. 'A paycheck every week while I play with my son.' To a twenty-seven year old mother who had never been trained to hold her own in the working places of the world, that seemed an absolute joy. 'And to think that a couple of months ago, I was in the hospital!'

★

She could see it all again. Three months before, she had been lying in yet another bed in a sterile hospital; Pamela remembered looking around at the attempts which had been made by the decorators to make the patients happy. Sunny yellow draperies with emerald green accents graced the large windows which overlooked the fronds of palm trees. She knew that beyond that immediate view one would be able to see the distant mountains, at least Camelback Mountain, providing all the buildings and traffic didn't obliterate one's view.

She didn't know exactly how long she had been lying in this particular bed, but the muscles and incisions, screaming at any slight movement, caused her to think that it had not been very long. True, she had been told of her long stay in intensive care, and she could vaguely remember someone standing over her bed in the darkness, whispering, "Come on, Pamela. You can make it." And, the memory was odd because every time it came, she thought of amethysts and blond curls, not knowing why.

She and her son had been on their way to Tucson, that Easter morning, to join friends for her favorite holiday which always had thrilled her with the scent and pure beauty of traditional Easter lilies, the gaiety of Easter egg hunts, picnics of ham and potato salad in the parks, and traditional church hymns sung en masse in the quiet beauty of stained glass and golden crosses. But, as fate would have it, they had not reached their destination. Only one block from home, someone had run a red light, smashing into

Pamela's red Torino, zeroing in on the driver's side squarely into her door. She remembered the sensations which had filled her as she first looked to the left when starting to cross the intersection. Instead of being able to see up the street, the grill of a silver Cadillac had obstructed her view. It was so close, she could have reached out and touched it had there been time. Seeing it was simultaneous with impact, it had surprised her at the time that she had felt no fear, heard no sound, and that she seemed to be seeing a movie in slow motion. The window and dash had started buckling and cracking silently into a peak of slivers above the rear-view mirror. Her hands had popped off the steering wheel as if an angry god had grabbed them and flung both backwards toward her head. Her body had been caught in a powerful force twisting it into a forty-five degree angle from the waist. Her trunk and legs held straight as if in a vice. Her upper body and face had slammed onto the front seat, protecting her features from flying glass, but shattering her spleen and bruising other organs and muscles. Bouncing back and being twisted ninety degrees in the opposite direction, tendons pulled from her rib cage and completed the damage to her body.

Slamming down onto her back, she had slid the length of the seat into the passenger's door where she lay helpless but aware that somehow she must stop the car, for it seemed as if it had developed a mind of its own and even then was starting to creep slowly across yet another intersecting street into only God knew what.

'I've got to reach the keys or the brakes, or we will be hit again broadside from the oncoming traffic which still has a green light.'

But her feet and arms would not respond to her mental prompting. Amazed that she was still alive, she heard her son call, "Mommie! Mommie!" and could feel his breath on her left hand as he peered over the front seat.

"Bury your face on the back of the front seat and hang on, Davie!" she commanded with what force she could – a whisper, for all of a sudden, when she went to take another breath, there was no ability with which to draw the air.

Unconsciousness had swept over her and it had felt as if she were spiraling through velvety black darkness toward someone who was waiting above her. She recognized the presence as that of her grandfather, whose pet she had been until he had died ten years earlier. Overjoyed, and not feeling pain any longer, she also became aware of a warm yellow light starting to radiate near her. The glow increased in loveliness and warmly cast a breath of sunshine over her. Her attention had become completely captivated by the ever-brightening phenomenon. Love for God filled her being.

Suddenly, a little forlorn voice, traveling through the blackness which had just marked her passing, caught her awareness. She could hardly hear it.

"Mommie! Mommie! Don't die! Please don't die!" the voice broke into a sob.

Pamela had felt momentarily confused. And then she remembered, 'My son. I have a son. I can't cop out now. The poor boy doesn't even have a father... but, I can't breathe!'

And then, remembering the experience she had just had, she beseeched, 'Jesus, help me. Please help me,' for she felt that He was near.

Simultaneously with her plea, she felt something stir in the right part of her chest. It filled her esophagus and mouth. She was able to breathe with little agonized gasps. She felt a dull thud and heard the engine of the car whine as the vehicle slowly came to rest nose first in a wire fence which surrounded a schoolyard. The sounds of sirens had filled her ears, and a burst of sunshine splashed into her eyes as the door above her dangling head opened. A fireman, who looked surprisingly like her father, looked into her pained grey eyes.

"Oh, little lady!" he had softly said as tears welled into the blueness which gave her hope. Wiping the back of his capable hand across his eyes to rid them of the moisture, he instructed others whom she could not see, to assist him in sliding the stretcher under her wrenched body.

"Be careful. It looks like she has a broken neck," he quietly instructed, as many pairs of hands attempted to hold her in a steady position.

The movement of their efforts caused her air supply to completely stop.

"Please," she whispered, "I can't breathe."

"You mean you can't breathe when we slightly raise you?"

"Yes," she gasped, and then everything seemed to go very far away again. Moments later she rebounded and saw that the car was positioned ahead of her at a crazy angle, looking as if it had grown four times its size, dwarfing herself who had become a midget. "Where's my son?" she breathed from the ground on which the stretcher now lay.

"Look right up there, Miss. Don't move your head." And, indeed, she could not, for it had been bound fast to protect the vertebrae. She looked straight ahead, raising her eyes as instructed. There Davie stood. Nine years old, blond shock of soft hair hanging above his eyes, wet lines shimmering on his little face. Their eyes met... his green melded with hers of grey. She smiled softly at him, reassuring that all would be well.

The next thing she knew, was that of being lifted into the back of a red van. Someone lying beside her was crying loudly for her mother. Pamela's arm was extended across the distance between them. Without moving her head, she could see that it was a young woman of her own age. She had apparently been the driver of the other car.

"Mother! I want my mother!" the stranger loudly screamed and sobbed.

"Lady, I know that you are hurt, but your injury is only superficial. If you don't quiet down and behave so we can tend to this girl she will die before we get her to the hospital. Please help us keep her alive by being quiet!" the medic firmly implored.

Pamela was watching the blond woman whose tears were coursing down her cheeks. She caught the girl's eye and whispered, "I'm sorry. Here, take my hand and let's pray positively together that we will be all right."

The blond lady reached over and closed her fingers around Pamela's braced, outstretched hand which had been jammed into that position during the accident. Pamela's consciousness faded.

The medic worked over Pamela to keep her breathing. She felt herself being lifted again. The pain was intense. She fell into darkness... moving... moving... people excitedly ordering others out of the way.

When she awakened, her eyes were looking into those of her little boy's and those of her best friend, Jill Farthing, who was smiling tearfully down at her. The warmth of her friend's feelings toward her tugged at her heart and she wanted to cry, but the emotion threatened to stop her breath again. Instead, she thought of her soldier husband as if he were alive until she was able to project her thoughts to the more recent memories of Jill and herself grubbing and slaving at secretarial, hostess and modeling jobs to support themselves and little David before she finally landed a job as a designer in an architectural firm.

In spite of not having all the amenities one would wish for, they all had loved each other and cheerfully forged a good life for themselves out of sheer will-power. 'Never say die!' had been their motto and often it had been repeated with genuine humor over the ridiculousness of various situations,

'But this accident! This was too much!' so thought her friend as she looked down at Pamela. The pinkish fluid accumulating in the bottles hanging on the stretcher worried Jill. 'Thank goodness her face and body aren't scarred; that is obviously blood in those containers,' she thought. X-rays clearly showed that a shattered spleen and other internal injuries were responsible for the seepage, not to mention the collapsed lung which had to be mechanically inflated.

Pamela had hung between life and death for several days following surgery. The pain in her body matched the pain in her heart when she heard the doctor ask if she wanted her husband to come.

"He's dead," she softly whispered as she choked to suppress the longing ache in her heart. How she had loved him. She had wanted to die when she learned of the crushing resistance during the Tet Offensive in Vietnam which had snuffed out his young life. But now that death was truly facing her as well, she wanted to live to raise their son.

Recuperation proved to be a slow process. Upon release from the hospital, her doctors advised that she refrain from work for another year. Faced with the impossibilities of raising a child with no support, she had decided to work anyway. And, so it was that her sensitive boss had offered her the rest which he knew the surgeon had prescribed. Another reason also lent itself to his proposal.

★

Pamela rolled over in bed feeling drowsy from reminiscing. Falling asleep, she started dreaming that she was floating in a small fishing boat on a lake. Her son's father had taken them to the spot for a bit of summer fun. Helping Pamela and Davie into the boat, he released the binding rope from the dock, readying his right foot to step into the boat, when suddenly a massive gust of wind and rain hit them full force. A sheet of water washed between her husband and the boat, subsiding over an empty dock. Looking for her son's father, Pamela grabbed her son into her arms, sheltering him with her body while struggling to climb over the seat to take hold of the steering device on the motor which was slamming back and forth crazily against the frame. She didn't have time to secure lifejackets on her son nor herself although they lay in the bottom of the boat next to the motor along with the rest of the fishing gear.

The boat had already been swept far from shore. She shoved her son between her knees, ordering him to grab around her waist and to bury his face on her midriff. He knelt before her, doing as she ordered while she frantically pulled on the rope which was supposed to ignite the motor. She tried and tried but couldn't make the rope uncoil fast enough to spark the plugs into a start. In desperation she let go of it, took hold of her son, and they both crawled on their bellies over the seat to the next one where she again positioned him.

She took hold of the oars and lifted them over the side of the boat into the heavy waves. At first they didn't even touch water, the swells were so deep and high. Finally, the oars touched, and she tried desperately to turn the boat into an angle which would keep them from capsizing. An angry wave came dashing at them from behind the boat, split into two factions, racing on each side of them, sweeping the oars away in a fury. Pamela's heart sank in despair as she grabbed the sides of the boat with her hands to steady the weight of herself and her son against the violent bucking. Her arms screamed with pain from tired, overused muscles. Her son's arms were weakening as he tried to clutch around her middle strongly enough to keep from being washed away from her in the froth and foam which angrily hissed around them.

All of a sudden, as dreams go, a blond-headed stranger appeared in the boat, back by the motor. He looked at her with calm violet eyes, threw lifejackets across the seat to her and turned his attention to the motor which was miraculously still banging away. He worked feverishly to clear the choke, wrestling against the wind and lurching of the vessel which would crest the six foot waves only to drop into the yawning, watery chasms below. Suddenly the motor kicked in and the stranger guided the battered boat into position so that it would be driven with the wind instead of broadside to the gale.

He then looked over at Pamela and her son. Pamela had managed to secure Davie into a lifejacket, but as she was about to don hers, she noticed that the stranger had given her the only other one in the boat, leaving himself without.

She tried to shout to him, tried to make him hear as she held the jacket out to him. He looked into her eyes, shook his head no, smiled and winked one eye in merriment as if nothing was wrong. Just then, the wind stopped and the boat was already docked, and the three of them were standing on solid ground high above what had threatened to be a watery grave but which was now a calm, blue lake sparkling in sunshine. She felt good, happy and secure; and in reality, slept the rest of the night undisturbed.

The next morning an excited Davie and Pamela boarded a jet homeward bound, leaving a disgruntled Ned DeSilva and happy, innocent Jill waving from the gate.

Chapter Two

From the busy streets of Central and Camelback in Phoenix to the quiet lanes of her father's farm in northwestern Minnesota was a welcome change for Pamela. The village was only a mile away, quaint and small, with homes shaded by cool elms and maples, surrounded on all sides by farms and gentle hills which looked as though they were freshly painted by Grant Wood. Life was easy going and gentle amongst the good folk. The townspeople were always ready to welcome a son or daughter who had been born and raised among them regardless of how far various ventures had taken them after graduation from the local red brick high school. In Pamela's case, she had gone away to attend the University of Arizona in Tucson. While there, she had met and married her son's father. A decade of happiness had followed.

Now, healing from physical and emotional trauma, it was good to lie in bed of a night, hearing only owls hooting or frogs predicting rainfall within twelve hours by their throaty croaking. She joyed in listening to the rustle of the leaves on her favorite elm tree outside the bedroom window as she lay trying to fall asleep. Even though the injuries sustained in the accident had healed for the most part, her endurance could not match the energy which she sometimes felt at this point.

'I need to get out and go swimming' she thought to herself. 'The doctor said that it would do a world of good in restoring my strength. Think I'll just go and do that tomorrow.'

The next day, she grabbed her swimsuit and with son in tow, headed for the little butterscotch Pinto which replaced the totaled Torino.

Out at the lake sailboats were breezing along off shore, drawing impatient looks from the fishermen who were sitting quietly in their stilled boats trying to catch a few fish. Just when they thought the line had a few bites, a speedboat pulling two skiers raced by. The group was whooping, laughing and having a wet and wild good time. To Pamela's surprise, the boat veered toward shore, slowed down and came sliding carefully beside the huge tractor innertube on which she and her son were floating.

"Hi there," grinned another kid about the size of Davie. Bobbing in the water, holding his skis so they would not strike his partner in the head, the boy said, "My name is Lance. This is my brother, and we were wondering if you are Mr. Deerfield's daughter and grandson."

"Why, yes we are," replied a surprised Pamela.

"Hey, Lance! Aren't you going to introduce your uncle?" a deep voice laughed from the boat.

"Oh, sorry," he shot a proud glance at the blond driver.

Pamela followed Lance's look and found herself staring into the most unusual set of violet eyes she had ever seen. Set like amethysts into a tanned face under a shock of blond curls, they seemed to flash with hidden lights when he looked into Pamela's startled gaze. Something ignited in that split second, causing her to catch her breath. She felt a wave of dizziness wash over her as a moment of déjà vu carried her in its arms, reminding her faintly of the hospital and the odd dream she had experienced before leaving Phoenix.

She felt her face flush as his attention slowly slid down to her bare shoulders to the black bodice of her bathing suit, taking in her voluptuous breasts, tiny waist, flat stomach, nicely shaped thighs, knees and ankles.

"You even polish your toenails," he observed casually as her coral tipped toes glinted through the clear water where her feet were propped against the opposite side of the tube from her torso.

Not knowing what to say in response to that observation, she was happy to hear Lance butt in, "Hey, fella, what's your name?" he looked at Davie.

"I am Davie Ellis and this is my mother, Pamela," he shyly answered.

"Well, how would you like to try skiing with us?"

"Oh, boy! Could I, Mom?" and he jumped off the innertube forgetting how deeply they had drifted, sank beneath the waves, and came spluttering back to the top. Laughing and half choking, he grabbed the tube, and shook the water out of his eyes. Everyone couldn't help but laugh along with him.

"Hey, Tiger, grab hold of my hand and let's go for a ride!" The muscle-bound man in the boat reached down with a mighty arm and hand, grasped David's small one in his and helped him climb into the boat over the side.

"Does the mother of this young man want to come along, too?" The Adonis looked down with a wink at her.

"Well, if I am allowed to get into the boat from off the dock, yes, I would enjoy a boat ride. I've not gone boating for years!"

"O.K., meet you at the dock," and he slowly pulled the boat forward so as not to hurt the boys nor dig into the golden sand on the lake's bottom.

Sidestroking on her left side while pulling the innertube with her right hand, Pamela made progress toward the shallow water where she could stand on the bottom and push the tube to the dock. She could feel the incision in her midriff knitting a little, but remembering that the doctor had urged her to stretch and use the muscles, she determinedly worked her way through the water. Reaching the dock, she looked up. The sparkle in the violet eyes intently watching her sent electrical charges flowing from the middle of her chest to her entire body.

She felt weak-kneed and as if the lower portion of her hips and tummy were being licked by flames. She wanted him. It made her feel momentarily ashamed because she didn't know the man.

"My name is Rick," he said softly as he reached a hand out to take the tube from her. She gazed in wonder at the forearm which had thrust itself in front of her. She had never seen such a concentration of muscles between wrist and elbow before, and to make it even more fetching, the arm was tanned to a perfect golden brown from what appeared to have been manual labor under fair skies.

His large square hand purposely landed on her small, white one. Letting it linger, he pressured hers ever so slightly and then slowly slid his off, letting his fingertips follow each of her fingers to the tips of her coral nails. She involuntarily shivered in spite of the heat coursing through her body.

The hot sunshine which was reflecting off the water, playfully cast lights across the intense eyes which held her spellbound. He smiled down at her.

"Rick Jarvis," he finished the introduction, nodding his head.

"Oh," she weakly replied, as she steadied herself against the boat.

"You've been news in our town for a few weeks now and I am glad that you are here. It gives me an opportunity, which after seeing you the first time, I didn't want to miss!"

She looked questioningly at him. 'I wonder when and where that first time was?' she silently mused. He seemed oddly familiar, yet he was a stranger.

"Here, climb into the boat, and after a few spins to pleasure the boys on their skis, we'll go to my cottage and rustle up some dinner... that is, if you are free and would like to join us?"

Mixed emotions were coursing through her mind. Her body was saying yes, but her intuition was saying that if she had no intention of having any serious romantic involvements in this part of the country, she had better say no. She found herself reaching to grasp his extended hand nonetheless.

'This man helping me into the boat is not of light stuff made. He is all man, with a man's desires and needs. Obviously, he is single – he wears no wedding band; but why not, at his age?' she found herself wondering as she stepped into the boat, steadying herself with his sure hand.

She looked at Rick who was preparing a place on which she could sit. Orange lifejacket in hand, he again looked at her, sensing her gaze. Their eyes met, electric violet beckoning the cool grey. She quivered inside from his penetrating look, feeling as if the very soul of her was being exposed. To her consternation, she became somewhat short of breath as shivers of delight ran through her heart.

'Oh, dear God,' she prayed, 'you know that this man seems too much for me to handle already, and I've just met him. And yet, I feel safe because those eyes remind me of cessation from pain in the hospital. Why I don't know – I can't remember.'

Nervously, she sighed, giving vent to a sudden stab of pain in her left lung. 'It will be so good when those pains go away,' she thought.

Rick's presence recaptured her attention totally. Her abdomen churned. Looking helplessly as a kitten into Rick's eyes, she momentarily rebelled against his magnetism and screamed to herself silently, 'I don't *want* to fall in love! I want to go back home.' A moment of déjà vu gripped her, which she resisted again as he held an orange lifejacket out to her. She tried to resist the strange feeling. The dream. The dream.

"Are you all right?" he asked. "You've turned pale as a ghost. Here, let me help you." and he gently led her to a seat beside his own. He leaned his backside against the steering wheel for a moment as his calm eyes studied Pamela.

"Oh, pardon me, I'm O.K., just remembered something and it startled me," Pamela explained, feeling like an absolute idiot.

With those thoughts in mind, she took hold of the life jacket and started slipping it over her head. Rick moved closer asking, "May I?" and slowly started to put the life preserver over her head, adjusting it on her shoulders. Together they fastened the straps, her shoulders feeling newly bare beneath his strong fingertips. His touch was as water to a person dying of thirst. She nodded her head, still feeling a little foolish and very exposed, especially now that her body in its tight bathing suit was no longer partially hidden by the water.

Soon, self-consciousness faded as she became absorbed in the fun and shouts of laughter which the two boys and her son were whooping up as they followed in the wake of the speeding boat.

The air felt good as it forced itself through her curls, causing her bright sweet hair to float thickly around her head. Slowing down, a mass of curls bounced forward, cascading around her oval face and neck. She brushed some of it out of her eyes to look back at Davie, who laughingly was sinking into shallow water as they glided slowly toward a dock she hadn't seen before. Tossing bronze-tinged curls off her shoulders, she looked questioningly at the man sitting beside her.

"I take it that you are going to have something to eat with us, and I won't take no for an answer," Rick purred as he bent over to speak softly into her ear.

She couldn't help but laugh at his impudence. "Making up my mind for me already, are you?" she teased.

"Yes, I am. And, what's more, I like it!"

"In that case, Sir, may I caution you not to do it too often, or you will probably meet the other part of me which can bite?"

"I can't imagine you biting anyone except for a playful nip on occasion."

Shocked, she looked at him, feeling her face turn hot and red as currents of fire reawakened in the depths of her body.

"You're terrible!" she injected, but there was such a comical look on his face at seeing her blush, she couldn't help but smile. The boat nudged the side of the dock.

Thankful for the interruption, she grabbed the rope tied to the supports of the platform, and hastily climbed out,

The boys and Rick busily secured the boat to the dock, then gathered skis, lifejackets, ropes, etc., and scrambled out of the water to climb up the sloping lawn to the log cabin on top of the hill.

A movement caught Pamela's eye. Rick had sprinted ahead, chasing after his two nephews who had already reached the cement steps leading into the cabin. There on the steps, standing as pretty as you please, were two of the most darling little girls Pamela had ever seen. One was as blond as sunshine, and the other was raven-headed with big eyes which looked luminous even from that distance. The blond was jumping up and down, squealing, "Rick! Rick!" and the ringleted, dark beauty was shyly staring past her uncle at Pamela who was slowly following behind. Rick and the boys reached the steps.

Rick, exuberant at seeing his nieces' joy, stopped at the bottom of the steps, holding his arms out to the little girls.

Davie nudged Pamela. "Look, Mom. Girls!" And he made a wry face.

She bent down and popped a light kiss on his forehead, feeling his wet hair under her lips. Ruffling the damp stuff with her hand, she said, "Is that bad? I'm a girl, too, you know."

"Oh, Mom, that's different," he groaned.

Rick, as if beckoned by their thoughts, turned. Grinning proudly, he held the blond in one massive arm, and the shy violet-eyed brunette in the other. Turning exuberantly toward Pamela and Davie, he asked, "How do you like my little sweethearts? This is Sandy, my fair-headed damsel, and this is Robin, my dark-headed baby!"

"Oh! You both are beautiful!" Pamela exclaimed, looking into their wide eyes.

"And you, Mr. Jarvis, are so fortunate to be fathering such lovely girls!"

The blond giggled, "Oh, but he isn't our father. He's just our uncle!" and with that she laughed even harder at Rick's quick response.

"*Just* your uncle, is that it! You stinker!" The little girl grabbed his face between her chubby hands and kissed him soundly on the cleft of his square chin.

An hour later, during the course of a fresh fish and French fried potato meal, Pamela learned that Rick was closely knit with the four children. Excited chatter and laughter included David and herself throughout the meal, making them feel completely at home. Finishing with huge dishes of chocolate ice cream, the kids excitedly excused themselves from the table, and ran out to play Kick-the-Can, a game of hide-and-seek best suited for playing after nightfall.

Suddenly, the room became quiet. Pamela started rising, taking her plate and silverware in hand. Rick gently touched her hands and said, "Leave the dishes this time, O.K.? I'd love to become better acquainted with you." Pouring two Grand Marniers into crystal aperitif glasses, he led her across the large room to the stone fireplace. Settling on a cushion in front of the fire, she accepted the proffered glass from Rick.

Sipping silently, she watched him turn and walk to the herring-bone couch on which he arranged his lean, muscular body.

Facing her and the fire, lights played across his face and hair. As he looked at her, Pamela thought that she had never seen anyone with such kind eyes except for her father's.

Rick started to talk slowly. Carefully, as if not wishing to disturb the memory of the woman whom he had chosen to marry three years previously, he was drawn by the compassion in Pamela's eyes into narrating the entire story. A few days before the wedding, his fiancées capillary disease had suddenly re-activated. She had died quickly during an acute attack of Lupus. Overwhelming grief had engulfed him, and in an effort to soothe the sting of losing her, he had organized The Lupus Foundation in which he took an active part soliciting public support.

"I am fortunate to have a brother as a doctor who is particularly interested in different forms of cancer. He and his wife, who is an R.N., have been a great encouragement to this program in the United States as well as in helping Third-World countries provide medical assistance for their unfortunate peoples. As a matter of fact, that is how I have ended up sharing their four children, whom you can see I thoroughly enjoy!"

"Yes?" Pamela encouraged. Rick shifted his lean frame, resting both elbows on his knees.

"Well, six months ago, Don and his wife were asked to embark on a relief mission to one of the nations on the African continent. They didn't know whether or not they should accept the assignment since it would mean leaving the children behind for a few weeks.

But, when I enthusiastically volunteered to keep the kids with me, they finally gave in and decided to accompany the medical supplies. They left four weeks ago and hadn't been there more than ten days when a coup d'état took place. They've not been heard from nor seen since. I haven't told the children yet because the State Department has assured me that there is every reason to hope for their recovery because a few days ago their effects were found near a rebel stronghold. It is our guess that they've been conscripted into caring for the wounded troops *and* civilians."

"Oh, Rick! How will you ever get them back?" Pamela breathlessly asked.

"If they are found, negotiations will begin to secure their release, and if that fails, other measures will be taken to spirit them out of the country to safety. I pray to God that they will be returned safely, but (and he cleared his throat) if they aren't, I'll be more than happy to adopt these four children. I've always been crazy about them as it is." His golden head dropped slightly as he soberly studied the crystal glass in his hands.

Pamela felt her heart strangely stirred as she listened to his poignant narration. During the hour and a half that it had taken for him to quietly bare his soul, she had become completely captivated by whatever it was that had first reached out to her that afternoon upon their meeting on the lake.

Rising slowly to go to him, not knowing what she was going to do, nor how, she fought the urge to kneel before his bowed head.

He was poised on the edge of the cushions, elbows on knees, both massive hands holding the fragile stemware by its dainty cup. She hesitated, shyness suddenly overpowering her feelings. She walked silently to the other side of the mantel, and placing her glass on its deep brown surface, asked quietly, "And, where is your home, Rick?"

"I have a farm located a few miles west of town. Would you like to come out to see it tomorrow?" his eyes brightened as he raised his head to look at her.

Pamela thought for a moment. "It's so nice of you to ask, but I must go to the clinic in Fairgate tomorrow morning."

"Well, that is a thirty-four mile ride one way," he said. "What time will you be finished?"

"It shouldn't take long. Perhaps I will be able to leave the clinic by 10 a.m. at the latest. I asked for an early appointment," she smiled.

"You still could stop by my place on your way home," he figured. "You'd have plenty of time to see every facet of my dairy operation if you used the county back roads as short cuts to return home. It wouldn't even be out of your way."

"That sounds good, but I do need to be home by the time Davie gets out of summer school," Pamela softly fenced.

"Why don't you just have him get on our school bus and ride home with my four? The littlest lady will be in kindergarten tomorrow, too. She goes three times a week."

His meaning was obvious. They'd have most of the day together alone, providing she returned in time herself. Not knowing whether or not that was such a good idea in lieu of the deep feelings which had been stirred in her for the first time in two years, she asked, "Will your work be hampered by having a guest all afternoon?"

Rick smiled again, coyly figuring out why Pamela was being a little elusive of being pinned down. "No, I'll just put my guest to work if she'll bring her jeans and boots along," he merrily announced.

Pamela said a silent, 'Touché,' and, aloud, "O.K., I will definitely stop by. And, now perhaps I had better go call Davie. We really ought to be going home." She crossed over the polished floor and started to pass in front of him to get to the porch. It had been hard to loosen herself from the magnetism of his unusual eyes, but feeling very hungry sexually, Pamela had purposely roused herself from the feeling of togetherness which had been caressing them. As she passed by, she felt herself being gently grabbed around the waist by two strong hands.

"Not so fast," he softly said and pulled her down. Waves of dizziness washed over her senses. She couldn't have stood if she wanted to.

Rick's lap felt warm and hard under her skin. Not having any clothing along other than the suit in which she had been swimming, Rick had given her a shirt of his own to wear. The tails of the shirt hung halfway to her knees, which made her feel clothed. But now, the tender places behind her knees were in direct contact with the perfect golden-haired maleness of his firm legs. Her veins became hot paths of liquid flame.

"Let me go. Please," she whispered. Her heart was beating so loudly that she thought surely he would be able to hear it, too. Wild passion soared through her body as she struggled to keep her composure,

"Don't fight me," he softly breathed into her ear. "You feel exactly the same way as I. Why pretend that you don't?"

She shut her eyes helplessly, yearning to make the world go away just for a moment of bliss with this compelling stranger.

"We aren't children anymore, and I dare say that it has been just as long for you as it has been for me since we have felt like this. People just don't fall in love with everyone they meet," Rick persuaded.

He adjusted her in his lap so that she was cradled in his left arm. Toying with a button on her borrowed shirt, he asked, "Isn't that so?"

Looking squarely into his eyes which were so close to hers for the first time, she was surprised to see the gentleman in him smiling out at her. Not the taker, but the patient man was again obvious. Her fear melted. "Yes," she timidly replied.

Shutting her eyes momentarily to hold back the tears which his obvious concern suddenly caused, she tried to guide their thoughts back to other things.

"It touches me to realize that you are so willing to care for your four nieces and nephews." That not being the real reason for them, another tear slid unchecked down her cheek. He reached up and carefully wiped it away with his thumb as he held her sweet face gently in his hand. In a sudden release of confidence to a man for the first time since her husband had been taken from her, Pamela continued, "I always wanted six children, but it was never meant to be." Another tear slid down her alabaster cheek. "And even though I would never trade Davie for anything nor anyone in this world, I couldn't have more children after he was born." More tears joined the first, but she did not sob as she allowed herself to be carried into a deeper vein of grief which had been tapped into compassion for Rick while listening to his story of losing the woman he had loved. Thinking of the coincidences which joined this enchanting stranger to her own awareness, she nevertheless dwelt verbally on her son.

"Davie is the only light in my life which has never gone out. I'd die if I lost him, too." And then, the underlying core of pain which had been buried after her husband's untimely death came out in hesitant agonized words.

Never before had she spoken openly of her loss, for to speak of it would surely allow her wild agony to run unchecked in front of those who couldn't possibly understand the tearing in her depths which threatened to reach up and rip her mind to shreds.

In an effort to protect herself from devastation by the cyclone of despair which lay buried deeply within her, she had submerged it in a whirlwind of activity. Now, sitting on this gentle stranger's lap, she felt kindred in spirit with him, a liaison born of the tragic experiences which had visited them both. She felt that his strength could safely shelter her if she dared give in to the urge to cleanse her heavy soul of its awesome load. Quivering ever so slightly as she looked into his kind face, words slowly formulated, spilling over trembling lips into the clarity of shared thought for the first time.

"We were so happy, so optimistic in spite of the imminent disaster which was waiting to separate us. He died in Vietnam... my husband." She softly wept. "Why did he have to be in that particular battalion? Other troops survived, why didn't my husband?" Raising her troubled eyes she looked deeply into his, whispering, "I know exactly the pain you must have experienced when your fiancée died. I wish I could erase your sorrow because if it is anything like mine, it hurts so wickedly."

"There... there... Kline Traub," he gently crooned, rocking her slightly in his strong arms.

Shaking from the effort to control the wellspring of grief which was gushing as freely as an artesian well for the first time, she continued, "Losing someone irretrievably hurts so terribly! I can't bear to think that you have experienced the same devastation, too."

Fresh tears coursed down her face. "Oh, dear!" she suddenly said with embarrassment. "Here I am pouring out my woes to a perfect stranger." Valiantly trying to smile through the salty wetness on her lips, she smiled, trying to buck up under the load of memories.

"But I have seen you before, Kline Traub," he whispered. She felt momentarily confused and looked bewilderedly into his eyes. His hand left her waist, and she felt his arms tenderly encircling her, completely folding her into his warm chest. She buried her face in the warmth of his body which smelled fresh and clean of lake water. He bent to kiss the top of her vibrant soft hair as he felt warm tears soaking through the linen of his shirt. "Kline Traub, Kline Traub," he whispered over and over until her sobbing subsided. She had not felt so protected nor cared for in such a long time, and her senses relaxed in his healing touch.

"I know how you feel," he whispered as he pulled her head gently from his chest to a wide expanse of shoulder. "Sometimes life can became overwhelming, but invariably, there seems to be a light at the end of the tunnel, don't you agree?"

What he was saying made sense to her. Yes, if she had not experienced loss, she would not have been ready to experience this new gain in her life. By the same token, had Rick not experienced losing his loved one by death, he would not have been prepared to share the full measure of her sorrow,

'Neither of us would have been ready to meet one another,' she thought to herself as she allowed herself to be comforted into peace.

The man holding her so tenderly was unusual in that he had already picked up on her deepest feelings, sharing them completely. She fleetingly thought of Ned, and of how shallow his interest in her was in comparison to this meeting of the spirits which she was experiencing with Rick. In spite of the bitter past, she felt joy at having met this sensitive, new friend with whom she could share. For the first time in two years, someone's immediate presence overshadowed the longing for a lost love. Something new was quickening within her being, and she welcomed it, finally, and at last.

Timidly she whispered, "What does Kline Traub mean?"

Cozying her little head into the welcome slight scratchiness of his neck and chin, he smiled and said, "It is a German phrase meaning 'little dove'. My father used to comfort Mother with those words when she was heartbroken over something... she was a tender English woman." He gently caressed her shoulder.

They sat quietly, contemplating their new-found friendship, dreamily gazing into the glowing coals of what had been a roaring fire. The children's laughter evoked by happy games came floating in to them, mingling with the call of a loon and the gentle lapping of small waves against the lakeshore. The changing shadows and faint light created by the dying embers, exposed the burnished copper tones in Pamela's dark hair, making it look warm and alive. Rick reached up to touch it, it looked so thick and inviting.

It proved to be as soft under his fingertips as he had imagined, and feeling suddenly aroused, he knew that if he were to remain a gentleman and not scare this wounded little dove on his lap away, he needed to disentangle himself and take her home across the lake. Silently to himself he said, 'I do want to see you again, little one. And, I want it to become such that I will never have to take you home and leave you there for the night again. I don't dare tell you yet, but you are what I have been waiting for these three, long and lonely years.' So musing, he asked if she thought that perhaps it was time for the children to be gathered, and taken to their beds, which involved a six mile trip in both cases.

"Yes," Pamela murmured, as Rick's warm lips gently touched her own. Like a leaping flame of fire, their innermost beings ignited, and suddenly the kiss became deep and urgent in its giving and receiving. Gasping, they both wrenched apart at the same time, trying to control the passion which was overwhelming them. Firmly putting Pamela from the circle of his arms, he helped her rise from his lap to a standing position. She swayed, and he leaped to his feet, catching her in his tanned arms.

"Are you not feeling well?" he worriedly asked, holding her away to look into her lovely grey eyes. Never before had he seen dove-grey irises which were edged with charcoal. It gave her eyes an enchantment and definition which was most disturbing because of their unusual loveliness.

Secured in pearly whiteness which was then fringed by thick, fine, black lashes, the windows of her soul looked trustingly at him.

"I will be fine. I just felt a little dizzy from all the crying, I sup-pose," she excused herself. 'Actually,' she thought silently, 'when I am around you, I feel as if I have known you all my life,' she smiled wistfully.

Taking her arm, Rick looked down at the little lady who looked charmingly dwarfed as she stood in his big shirt. He thought of the first time he had ever seen her as she lay in intensive care, he and his brother fighting to save her life. Silently he mused, 'Some day I'll tell you where I first found you, and how you ended up coming here for the summer – but not right now.' Aloud he said, "Let's go little lady," and again to himself... 'before I lose control;' and they went to call the children.

Chapter Three

The next morning Pamela hurried through the breakfast dishes, and scooted her son out the door with the last minute admonition to catch Bus #5 after school with Rick's nephews.

"I'll be out at his ranch," she said. "Won't it be fun to watch the dairy operation tonight?" She winked at him. "You've never seen a red barn full of cows, let alone seen where milk comes from! Did you know that one has to pump the tail in order to get the milk to flow?"

"Oh, Mom! That's not how you do it!" Davie exclaimed.

"How do you know?" she laughed as he went running out the door. Turning to run upstairs to get her purse, she took another sweet roll off the plate of breakfast breads which Elsie, her adopted aunt had prepared and left on the table earlier that morning. 'She sure makes good breads,' Pamela thought as she tasted its yeasty goodness. 'If I keep this up, I won't fit into my jeans at the end of the summer,' she worried as she heard the telephone ring. Setting the roll down onto a breakfast plate she delicately wiped her fingers on a napkin, and walked across the emerald carpeting to pick up the telephone receiver. To her delight, the caller was Mr. Randolph.

"Why, Mr. Randolph. How nice of you to call! Is everything all right?"

"Strange that you should ask," he chuckled. "As a matter of fact, that is why I am calling," he responded.

"How is that, Mr. Randolph?" Pamela continued,

"Well, as you know, I was negotiating regarding a new project prior to your departure. The clients have decided to accept my proposals and we will be starting work on it immediately."

"That sounds wonderful!" Pamela exclaimed. "They know quality when they see it, obviously," she smiled. "But, I thought you were on your way to England."

"I don't know about that first statement of yours, but I do know one thing and that is that this office has been utter chaos ever since you left. I almost regret having let you go for so long. Is there any chance that I could induce you to give me an answer regarding the proposed buying trip? I'd rather have your efficiency and charm along than what is presently available in your place." He chuckled.

"Isn't the temporary girl working out well? I thought she came very qualified and I've not worried about anything, thinking that all has been running smoothly for you."

"She does have her good points," Mr. Randolph replied. "However, it seems that she is more interested in her boyfriend than in her drawing board, or the typewriter for that matter."

"I'm sorry to hear that, Sir," Pamela said with genuine concern. "You certainly need someone who is on the ball in handling your affairs."

"Which brings me to my point, Pamela," he continued. "One word sums it up. *Help!*" and both parties burst into laughter.

"What will you give me if I come back?" she teased good naturedly.

"That's not the question. It should be, what will you get if you don't return!"

She burst into fresh laughter. "How about a million dollars?" she added ridiculously.

"Is that all? You sure don't believe in asking for much, do you," he rejoined,

Mr. Randolph had always been a good natured tease, and his friendship had filled Pamela with a zest for her job during the years in which she had worked for him,

"Seriously, Mr. Randolph, I would be honored to go to England with you but I also feel that I must stay with Davie who has decided not to go to camp this summer. He said that he wishes we could be together. Memories of the accident still plague him somewhat, and I guess he needs the security of having me near him for at least awhile. The doctor said that his fears will soon subside and he will not need reassurance out of the ordinary much longer."

Her boss's voice became very compassionate. "Well, Pamela, I can certainly understand that, and yes of course, you mustn't leave right now. Stay with the boy. That is most important at this point."

"Thank you, Mr. Randolph, and be sure that I did want to accompany you to England. Also, I feel terribly flattered that you chose me to go; and besides, I love to design around antiques you know."

"Yes, that is why you like to design around *me*," he dryly interjected.

"Oh, stop!" they both laughed. "You know that it makes the drawing board come alive to see objects of art in their original settings," she added wistfully. "Seeing them in their places of origin would enrich my acumen as to what looks good."

"I understand, dear. And, I too am sorry that you can't go along. However, first things must come first, and let's just be glad that you are still around to enjoy such things. I will see you soon as it is. Before you know it, the summer will be past, and we'll all be settled back into our boring routines."

"Never boring," Pamela countered.

"Well, I must run along. I leave for the bliss of antiquity a week from today. If you should think of anything which might enhance our image as the greatest firm in the Southwest, don't hesitate to call before I leave."

"O.K., Mr. R. And, take care. Thanks again for this summer with my son," Pamela said before thoughtfully replacing the receiver into the cradle.

She thought of all the interesting things which would be waiting for her at work once she returned to Phoenix in the fall. But, her thoughts became somewhat confused because interjected into them were flashbacks of Rick smiling, Rick comforting her, Rick, Rick, Rick. She knew that when the time came, it was going to be difficult to leave him and go a continent away. She already felt such a part of this new friend that she couldn't comprehend never seeing him again. It was as if she had found a long lost friend during their discussion the night before.

'How is this all going to work out?' she pondered as she started up the stairs to get her purse.

She decided to sweep her hair into a Gibson Girl and walked down the ancient hall toward her bedroom. The telephone rang again.

'This time I will answer on the phone in my bedroom,' she thought as she put a little speed into her stride. Lightly, she ran to catch the call before whoever it was could hang up.

"Hello?" she answered breathlessly.

"Good morning," Rick's voice came over the wires intimately into her ear. Goosebumps tingled up and down her arms from hearing his resonant voice which last she had heard as he had kissed her goodbye the night before. Hoping she didn't sound like a silly little girl, she nonetheless could not keep from giving in to the joy and exuberance his voice triggered. She felt so happy just *thinking* of him and returned the greeting by asking how he was feeling.

"After being with you yesterday, I am feeling better than I have in years, young lady. And, I trust that you are well rested and ready to make a dash to the clinic for your checkup by now?" he pressed.

Carefully securing her hair with the golden pin, she said, "Oh, yes! I feel just wonderful and can't wait to get out into the sunshine. The whole world looks absolutely glorious this morning."

"As I am sure you look also," his voice smiled over the phone.

Catching his little quip, she had to laugh, and teased him back before thoughtfully hanging up the receiver.

Hurrying so as not to be late for her appointment, Pamela dashed out of the door.

★

"Rick! Isn't this a darling calf?" Pamela exclaimed, as she thought of the past month, most of which every day had been spent with Rick at the ranch. They were standing in a calf barn which was a low slung extension of the larger dairy barn. The calf barn housed forty calves. Each calf boasted of its own compartment. The walls of every compartment were made of one-by-twelve-inch boards which were spaced evenly apart to allow good ventilation. Fresh straw carpeted each stall beneath the calves' tiny hooves. Rick had just finished nursing a greedy little Jersey which resembled a fawn minus its spots. The bucket which the man held sported a large black rubber nipple out of which a few drops of the mother's first milk was still dripping.

He pulled his boot off the lower one-by-twelve as Pamela observed aloud, "Mr. Randolph would be interested in seeing this bovine motel! It isn't exactly the architectural wonder of the age, but it certainly is functional and has been neatly and well made."

"Ah, yes. Your employer." Rick agreed.

Pamela cast a look of surprise at Rick, "How did you know that he is my employer?" she asked.

"Well," Rick drawled, "he is famous in his own right as an architect/designer in Phoenix who creates the most ingenious buildings and is rather in demand everywhere."

Rick looked at her keenly.

"He's married, is he not?" Rick pursued.

"Oh, yes. He has a lovely wife."

Two arms swept her away from the calf corral, squeezing playfully.

"I'm jealous of him, even if he is married," he kissed her greedily.

"Rick, what are you saying?" Pamela caught her breath. "You hardly know me and already you are becoming possessive? I won't be living up here forever you know;" and she pushed him away, realizing as she did so that they already knew one another more than most people do in a year as a result of their shared confidences during the past four weeks. She took off, sprinting down the aisle of the barn toward the haymow ladder.

"Come back here, you little cat!" Rick called, as she started bounding up the steps as fast as her tight jeans would allow. All of a sudden he was right behind her, grabbing at her ankle as she pulled it up the last step into the sweet hay which was spread on the wooden floor.

Laughing and pulling free, she scampered toward a long rope which was hanging from the peaked ceiling where it was attached to a large pulley. She jumped like a gazelle off the raised part of the floor over which she had been escaping Rick's chase. A stitch of pain in her midsection reminded her to be careful as she grabbed the rope. Running across the floor to the next platform which was still half-packed with bales, she gave a jump using her hands for leverage, and landed on her knees in the hay. Before she could stand upright to swing away on the rope as she had intended, Rick was right beside her. He grabbed her in his strong arms, and then fell laughing into the soft, fragrant bed of hay.

Pinned beneath his chest and left arm, she blew bits of hay and grass out of her mouth and brushed her hair from her eyes. Rick marveled at the cloud of chestnut hair which gleamed with coppery highlights in a shaft of sunlight which was streaming through the pigeon hole at the top of the haymow. He saw the golden pin with the cool, green jewel sparkling like deep water as it lay buried in the runaway Gibson hairdo. His violet eyes came to a glowing standstill, looking upon her closed eyelids. Slowly, sensing his mood, Pamela opened her beautifully fringed lids, exposing the bewitching charcoal-etched irises which utterly fascinated her admirer. Searching each other deeply, the laughter died away from her eyes as soft questioning lights started to glow deep within the grey orbs. Rick bent slowly to kiss her warm, inviting mouth. Soft lips lightly touched hers, lifted up and immediately claimed hers again, softly, softly. He kissed her lightly on the tip of her delicate nose, kissed each closed eyelid, traveled with his gentle kisses across her forehead to her temple, down to the lobe of her right ear.

"I love you," he whispered. "Marry me!"

The exquisite teasing of his light consistent touch did its work, and all resistance was dashed away.

"Oh, Rick! Darling, yes! Yes! I love..." and the rest of her sentence was engulfed by his lips reclaiming hers. She felt herself being lifted into a torrent of passion which traveled from her reeling head, flowing hotly downward like melted wax cascading slowly, deliberately down the sturdy stem of a burning candle. She wanted him.

'Oh, I mustn't, I mustn't!' she thought to herself and turned her head away. But, not put off so easily, he gently took hold of her head with his masterful left hand, and turned her face back to him.

"I haven't wanted anyone in three long years... not until I saw you three months ago as you lay in the Intensive Care Unit near death's door, my brother working feverishly to inflate your lungs. Now you are here in my arms promising to be in my life and I long to love again," Rick murmured.

In spite of the moment's passion, Pamela was astonished at Rick's disclosure.

"You were there?" she asked incredulously, feeling his warm lips tenderly kissing her brow.

"Yes, darling. I was there."

"But, I don't understand! How could you have been there, and for what reason?"

By now, all thoughts of whether or not she should make love to him had left her mind, except for the deliciously disturbing fact that his strong arm was still criss-crossed over part of her midriff and waist. Trying to ignore the sensations which hotly flooded inside of her from such close contact, she focused on the astonishing revelation he had just allowed to escape.

"I thought you lived here," she exclaimed weakly, trying to calm her beating heart. 'If he doesn't remove his arm, I am going to have to pursue this line of thinking another time,' she thought to herself,

Grasping his right shoulder to steady herself into an upright position, she frowned. Releasing her so that she could sit cross-legged in front of him on the hay, he teased the outline of a butterfly on her cowboy boot with a stray blade of wheat, then contemplatively brought it between his lips, biting on it with little nips between his snowy, even teeth. Spitting a piece of the yellow straw from his tongue in an aside, his penetrating eyes looked into hers.

"Yes, I first saw you at Doctor's Hospital in Phoenix when you were brought in on a stretcher. One of my brother's colleagues had been called away for a few days, so Don, my brother, called and asked if I could take the other fellow's place for the duration."

"But, you're a rancher, a dairy farmer! I don't get the connection. And, even so, personnel isn't usually recruited helter-skelter. Doctors aren't pulled out of a hat like rabbits." She looked at him in disbelief.

"Hey! Don't look at me like that!" he laughed and grabbed her at the nape of the neck drawing her in one quick movement to him for a swift kiss.

"Actually, it is very simple. Yes, it is true that I am a rancher, dairyman, what have you. But, it is also a fact that

I am a doctor as is my illustrious sibling. He and I are twins, and decided to become doctors. It's as simple as that. So, we went to the same colleges, did our internships in the same place, and were offered positions where we interned. I lived in the Phoenix area for quite some time practicing medicine – rather learning to practice medicine. Doctors just happens to be my Alma Mater, so to speak. I, when I left to live here, agreed to come pinch-hit when and if needed." He looked over at her with a twinkle in his eyes. The look on her face was one to behold; big eyes, absolute amazement coupled with the look of a cat caught with a canary... as if she didn't belong with him anymore... as if perhaps she should drop the prize and run.

"Hey, little lady," he said drawing her close once more, "isn't that O.K.?"

"Yes," she faintly answered, feeling a wave of dizziness sweeping over her from the nearness and scent of the man. She felt as if she were pleasantly swimming in the fragrance of clean detergent and softener which was coming from his shirt, mixing with earthy smells of leather, sage cologne, and cattle. "But, I must say that you are full of surprises."

"As long as the surprises don't hurt you, that is permissible, is it not?" he gently asked, tilting her head with a gently placed hand under her little chin. She looked at him with wondering eyes.

"While I was there," she whispered, "I remember someone entering the darkness which seemed to cradle me. It was a man. I didn't know him, but he pulled me into awareness saying, 'Come on, Pamela! Yon can make it.' And, for some reason I always remember the color of lavender in connection with that person... and later before coming to Minnesota, I had a strange dream about a man with violet eyes and blond hair who saved Davie and me."

A serious look passed like shadows through Rick's purple eyes as he too remembered the incident in the hospital.

Seeing the shadow of thought visiting him, Pamela caught her breath, sat bolt upright, asking, "That wasn't *you* was it?"

"Yes, darling. It was I," and he drew her to him again.

"But," she exhaled, "but..."

"When I saw the paramedics wheeling you into the emergency room, I had the same reaction as my brother who came later to take charge in the Intensive Care Unit. He said that when he pulled the curtain back to enter your compartment, he didn't expect to see such a beautiful young women lying there. His eyes filled with tears as he thought, 'What a waste! I don't know that I can save her.'

Don and I noted that your coloring had changed drastically, and you were bleeding internally, scarcely able to breathe what with only one lung operating partially. It was obvious that you were being weighed in the balance, and it couldn't be helped because lengthy preliminary examinations by X-ray had of necessity been given to ascertain the extent of your injuries." Rick sighed, shaking his head.

"The nurses and technicians told Don of your courage, and of how you had asked to be told what was found because the *not* knowing made you afraid and interrupted what little ability to breathe you still maintained. Most don't want to know, but I guess that is when I decided that you were the type of person I'd like to know. You have courage. And to top it off, you were absolutely sweet and caring about the personnel whenever you would regain consciousness, not to mention the crazy jokes you'd mumble while half out of your senses when the pain was so intense you'd pass out. Nope, honey, you were our special angel while you were in that hospital."

Pamela sat stunned, just looking at him. He could see moments of pain sweep through her grey eyes during certain parts of his narration, but for the most part, the look of surprise never left her face.

"Well, how did you happen to find me once I was up here?" she asked.

"Oh, that was easy," he grinned. "I already knew that you were coming," and a mischievous smile greeted still more amazement.

"What do you mean?" she queried.

"Well, that is something you ought to know also. Actually, my brother suggested to Mr. Randolph that you be given a few months off during which to recuperate. He agreed with the idea, and said that he would figure something out. No one wanted to see your health permanently impaired. Eventually, Mr. Randolph called my brother and told him that you had decided to come up here for the summer.

"My brother relayed the information saying, 'Well, your wish is now coming true.'"

"Had you told him that you wanted to get to know me?"

"Yes, I had told him," and with that he jumped to his feet, pulling her up beside him. Tugging her along to keep pace with him as he helped her clamber over bales, dips, and platform, he reminded her that chores don't wait. She accepted his help, noticing the strength and ease with which he handled her.

'Sure feels good to have a man looking out for one even in a simple effort like bale climbing,' she smiled to herself. 'It makes me feel so feminine, and I love it for a change!' "Oh! Romeo! Come sweep me off my feet!" and she laughed aloud as Rick turned to catch her in his arms. She jumped the three feet off the top of the bales down to the wooden floor near the chute through which bales were pitched to the stantions below.

"Hello, bossy!" she called, bending over to wiggle the fingers of her right hand at a curious cow who was chewing her cud in slovenly delight while taking in the sights above her head. A surge of happiness charged through Pamela's chest, and she gave Rick a dazzling smile.

"Don't ever let it be said that I impeded progress... let's go," and she scooted ahead of him down the ladder.

"Where should we go?" he teased, following behind her.

"I don't know. You're the boss... besides being the veterinarian!" she impishly laughed and jumped away to escape the swat of his hat which came off his head with amazing speed, grasped in one tanned hand.

"Veterinarian, huh?" and he ran the fingers of his left hand through his thick curls, settling the Stetson back squarely on his head.

Amethyst eyes, off-white hat, lavender Levi shirt with mother-of-pearl snaps set off Rick's masculinity.

"He's too handsome for his own good!" her breath caught in her chest.

Rick saw the admiration in her grey eyes which weren't frosted over by any lack of candor in that moment of private thought. He grinned, feeling ten feet tall and as if he had the whole world by the tail for the first time in ages.

"How would you like to become an assistant fence checker?" he shot an amused look her way as they proceeded down the aisle between bovine heads of registered quality.

Noticing one heifer suddenly jerking a tuft of hay loose from a section of bale which hadn't freed itself when thrown, Pamela looked up at her newly-acquired fiancé.

"Depending upon the benefits derived from such an endeavor, I don't think I'd mind a bit!" she jauntily exclaimed. "When do we start?"

"Right now, kid," and he swung open the door leading out to the stables. "Hmmmm, I might need these," he paused to sort a wire clipper out of a neat pile of recently used implements placed on the work bench above which was a neatly arrayed pegboard full of every kind of nail, clamp, screw, bolt, washer and nut she had ever seen.

"Looks like Sam has already been out on the back forty this morning," he said, noticing that certain tools had been used and left in a heap.

"Where's the back forty?"

"You sure do ask a lot of questions for such a little tadpole!" he gave her a sideways grin.

"Well, how else am I supposed to learn anything?" she shot back.

"You have a point there... which matches the top of your head," he mused softly, looking impishly at her with a quick glance.

"What do you mean by that remark?" she laughed, grabbing his hat off his impudent head.

"Hey! Come back here with that rain catcher!" and he reached out to catch her arm, but she was too quick for him and was already out the barn door running for all she was worth toward the stable. She heard his boots pounding in hot pursuit behind her, and felt a thrill of excitement surge through, making her run faster and laugh harder. She stretched her hand toward the door handle, but never quite reached it before being pulled backwards into strong, playful arms in a scramble to claim the stolen hat. Fits of laughter overtook both of them as she writhed around trying to keep the stolen goods. But, he was too big, and she was laughing too hard, and as his massive hand got a firm hold on the rim, he bent her over and kissed her until the laughter died. Feeling shaken to her boots by the hot fire he imparted into her veins, she felt herself responding, arms stealing sweetly up and around his neck. Feeling herself pressed against his pounding heart, she wished they were anywhere but standing in the middle of the yard.

"Oh, Rick," she caught her breath, and gently pushed him away as he nuzzled her with little kisses from her mouth up to her forehead.

"Let's go check fence," the words caught in his throat. Releasing her with his hand lingering on one elbow to guide her through, he opened the door. Walking over the threshold into the stables, an eager whinny greeted Rick.

"Hi, girl," he softly said, rubbing a beautiful chestnut mare's velvety nose and patting the side of her neck. The horse pushed her impatient head into the side of his neck, knocking his hat askew in the process. "Whoa, girl!" he laughed. "What are you looking for?" He reached into his pocket and took a couple sugar lumps from his jeans. Holding two of them on the flat of his palm, he held them out to her. Nodding and whinnying in pleasure, the horse curled her lips around first one and then the other greedily. Tossing her head up in delight, she chewed the lumps, coming back to lick the palm of his hand which was still outstretched toward her.

Fishing in his jeans for more, he asked, "Want to feed a sugar lump to my friend, Pamela?"

"Oh, Rick, maybe I'll pass."

"Come on. You will have to become acquainted some day and there is no better time than the present, don't you think?"

"Well, I guess not. Here," she said, "give me the lump, and we'll see which sugar she likes best, the lump or myself."

Rick laughed, "Well, if she has good taste, she will undoubtedly prefer you!" He reached an arm around her waist and drew her closer to his side, pressing tenderly against her, the side of his body as if a pillar bracing vertically between supple bosoms, down her midriff and tummy.

"Rick, the sugar lump?"

"Oh, yes. The sugar lump," and he took her right hand in his, lifted it to his mouth, kissing the palm. "I get to taste your hand before she," he murmured; "after all, I found you first."

Pamela smiled, and deftly bent over, kissing the knuckles of his right hand which was placing the sugar lump in her palm.

Closing her hand over the sugar, he looked deeply into her grey eyes. A sweet tenderness was emitting from them, a soft, electrical glow. It felt as if he could melt into the aura surrounding her which that particular look generated. For some reason he thought of soft pinks, cool greens, snowy whites and pale blues, The sunlight of her smile bathed him in warmth, and he felt as if for this he had waited, had lived through life without wanting anyone for three years. And, he knew that it had been worth the wait.

'I have never felt this kind of closeness and sense of belonging before.' he marveled. 'This is entirely new to me, and whatever it is, I love it. It feels as if Pamela is already a part of me, and as if she was meant to be with me.'

Thinking of how he had cared as deeply as he knew how four years earlier, he recognized that it hadn't been as complete, as beautiful, nor as comforting and exciting as his relationship with Pamela.

'There is a purity about this new love which I've never experienced before. It seems as if this girl is already bone of my bone. Yes, she seems as if she is not just herself but also a part of my very body and soul. And I have not as yet claimed her other than verbally. If it's this good already, what in the world will it be after that sweet moment?'

Studying him with eyes of love, Pamela noticed the thoughtfulness in the violet windows of his soul. The tenderness in them warmed her, making her feel secure and cherished.

Sweetly breaking away from the unexpected communion which enveloped them, Pamela turned to the mare, holding out her hand. The Arabian looked dubiously at the female form standing before the stall, gingerly touched her soft nose to the flattened, outstretched fingers and palm, and pulled her head upwards as if having been surprised by the scent of someone new.

"That a girl," Pamela softly crooned. "Don't be afraid, I won't hurt you. You are so pretty with that rich, deep brown coat, and soft nose. Come on my lovely lady, have another bit of sugar."

As if soothed by Pamela's soft voice, the skittish mare bent her head obediently, and delicately flicked the sugar lump out of the hand before her. Pamela smoothly reached up and started stroking the mare's warm neck, in soothing little strokes, unhurried, leisurely.

"That's a girl," she softly crooned. "Oh, I like you! You are quite a lady, aren't you. Yes, you are. And, what's more, you are an aristocrat, it is plain to see. Beautiful neck, flat croup, everything. You'd make any owner proud."

"Rick," Pamela exclaimed, "this mare is beautifully appointed. She must have a fine bloodline. She looks as gracefully delicate for a horse as a Jersey does for a cow. I'm surprised to find such a fine Arabian on a working ranch instead of being a brood mare elsewhere."

"Well, actually I did find her at just such a place. She was a filly, and I fell in love with her at first sight. It took quite a bit of talking to persuade my friend to part with her, but eventually it worked out to our mutual satisfaction. I didn't realize you knew anything about horses."

"Frankly, I don't know much about them other than I am captivated by their regal good looks such as this Arabian displays. I also am fascinated by the other types including quarter horses. I don't know why, but I especially love Indian ponies, too, you know – the brown and white pintos?"

Rick smiled at her preference for Indian ponies.

She went on to say, "I've always felt that if one had a good horse, one had a loyal friend also. They are intelligent, and can actually become an extension of one's own mind at times and *that* appeals to me. A good horse and rider make an excellent team, especially in ranch work or rodeoing."

"New word?" Rick grinned at the use of her last word.

Laughing together, they went to get the saddles and tack in the tack room. Rick stopped her in front of another stall to help her become acquainted with the horse which she would be using on her trips with him to the fields.

"Oh, this is a pretty little Palomino. Is she a quarter horse? Her build seems more squat than that of yonder statuesque beauty of slender legs and graceful hips."

"That she is."

"Well, I like her!" Pamela exclaimed. "Don't tell me that she is a prize winner, too. She's a little beauty for sure."

"She managed to come off with a red ribbon at the fair, but never has had quite what it took to capture the blue. She's a good barrel-racer and cow-cutter. She just goes ahead and does all the thinking for the rider when it comes to sorting cattle out of the herd. Because of that, I usually put one of the kids on her if I need extra help. She isn't high strung either, and doesn't shy nor bolt if a garden snake crosses her path, or some striped gopher comes streaking out of a hidden hole in the meadow grass. She's pretty even tempered, that little gal," and Rick stopped to introduce Pamela to her mount's habits when being saddled.

"Oh, I love her, Rick!" Pamela threw her arms around the pretty mare's head and neck, nuzzling her on the soft spot halfway down her nose. "We're going to get along just fine, aren't we girl," Pamela cooed.

The horse nuzzled Pamela back. They had become friends.

"You can rest assured that this little mare won't be throwing you. But, are you sure you ought to be riding yet, Pam? It's all right if I call you Pam isn't it?" He looked over at her and winked.

"Call me anything but miserable, and I'll not mind a bit. Rick, you have brought me such sunshine, and the incredible part about it is that I didn't know that I could use any more. I was already happy and had learned not to feel lonely nor blue about Davie's and my circumstances. As I saw it, I was so lucky to have my son, a good job, good friends – everything. But, now you have come along and added another dimension which surprises me. It has caught me totally off guard. I never believed anything such as this could happen to me so quickly, so intensely in such a short time. I used to mildly criticize others to myself if I was told that they fell in love within days, or at first sight."

"Why, darling?" Rick wanted to know.

"Well, I thought that love could only be learned, and that it was a mental process of getting to know someone intellectually first, and *then* the feelings of love would gradually make themselves known. That's how it happened to me the first time, and because I was that type, I thought everyone else was, too. Now, my theory has really been shot down, for this has happened to me and there is absolutely no rhyme nor reason to it. It's so wonderful," she finished breathlessly.

Rick took her in his arms, and gave her a sweet hug.

"You're absolutely something else, aren't you, sweetheart. There is such an innocence about you which is incredible for a twenty-six year old mother. I've been captured by it... an innocence and a purity which I have not noticed in other women whose appearances may have attracted me initially. But, once I learned to know them for a few hours or days, I was always disappointed in one way or the other. And then here you came. You are a fantastic woman!"

Chapter Four

"Which of us is going to check fence, and which milk cows tonight?" the good-looking hired hand hollered. He was standing, black hair shining shades of blue in the sunlight. His hair reminded Pamela of a raven's plumage, it was so extraordinarily rich. Simultaneously, Sam and Rick started walking across the yard toward each other as they talked. Pamela observed Sam's appearance and liked what she saw... black, thick hair, sky-blue eyes, a big mouth that liked to smile a lot and out of which was usually sticking a blade of Grandfather's Whisker's grass which looked like an over zealous shaft of wild wheat.

'The only difference between that weed and a stalk of wheat is that the weed forgot when to quit growing whiskers,' Pamela thought to herself.

"Howdy, Ma'am," Sam's pleasant voice drew her attention back to the men. He tipped his hat toward her and flashed a lopsided grin.

"Hi, Sam."

"When are you going to milk cows and do chores for Rick and me so's we can go chasen wimmen?" he drawled, aiming a wink at Rick.

The very thought of Rick chasing someone else sent an achy, sick feeling into the pit of her stomach. A twinge of unlooked for hurt pricked at her heart.

Keeping her composure, she said, "If you have to wait for me to help you go chase ladies, you are going to have a long wait," and she smiled cooly, wrinkling up her nose at Sam. "The pox on you!" she teased.

"What kind of hand are you – won't even take your turn so the boys can have a night out on the town," Sam plagued.

Pamela laughed, sauntering over to the men, hands partially in hip pockets, toe of boot tracing circles in the powdery dirt beneath her feet once she stood still. Noticing Sam's tan boots sporting hand-tooling almost to the toes, she wondered how a mere cowhand could buy such expensive footwear.

Looking up at the man, she couldn't help but like him in spite of his smart mouth, and she had a hunch that when he and Rick were alone, the vernacular between them became quite colorful. His blue straightforward eyes, his friendliness, and honesty was unusual. And, she noticed that there was something between the two men... she could feel it. Yet, Rick had never mentioned anything out of the ordinary, had always referred to him as his hired hand. But, the men seemed to be equals even though Rick was the leader when they were together. When alone, Sam was self sufficient and as capable a leader in his own right with everyone else other then Rick. They seemed inseparable, dearest of friends.

"I wish you could meet Jill," she found herself stating aloud.

'Oh, shut my mouth!' she winced to herself as soon as the words were out.

"And, who may I ask is Jill?" Rick also wanted to know.

"Yes, and are you also interested, Sam?" Pamela teased, Sam grinned.

"She's my dearest friend who lives in Paradise Valley," Pamela smiled. "Course, I don't know if I would trust such a gentle creature with Hot-Shot here." She looked up at Sam with head still bowed, peering through her feathery lashes.

Sam and Rick laughed rakishly.

"I don't think anyone should be trusted with this wild man," Rick laughed, slapping Sam across the shoulder.

Sam poked the blade of weed back into his insolent but good-natured mouth, looking at his friend in amusement.

"Oh, you wouldn't, huh?" he quietly smiled. "Well! Can't say that I blame you."

"So! Who is going to have the pleasure of playing nursemaid to forty Jerseys tonight? Chores have to get started in ten minutes, or their full udders will turn to cheese, and their tails will fall off."

Pamela looked at Sam, and asked, "Mastitis?"

Sam looked down at her with an amazed look of respect as he asked, "Where'd you learn about mastitis?"

"Oh, from the *Funny Farmer* magazine which was lying on the kitchen table in your clean ranch house the other day."

"What do you mean, *Funny Farmer?*" he laughed. "And what do you mean by that remark about a clean house? You think I'm a bad housekeeper, do you?" Sam wanted to know.

"No, just teasing," Pamela softly smiled.

"Hey, you two. We'd better get cracking here and get some work done. In answer to your question, pal, heads you do the milking and I do the fence-checking, tails we swap."

Rick fished in his pocket and drew out a quarter.

"What else have you got in there?" Pamela wanted to know as she darted her little hand into the warm depth next to his hip bone.

"Hey," he gasped, looking up to heaven, sucking in his breath.

Not realizing how sensitive an area she had inadvertently and thoughtlessly touched, Pamela blushed beet red and whirled about to hide her embarrassment from the laughing men.

"Oh, pardon me," she winced. "I didn't stop to think," and giggles started to scream for notice. Trying not to laugh so as not to appear a brazen hussy, she put her hands over her mouth.

Rick took her by the shoulders and turned her around. When their eyes met, she burst into a fit of embarrassed laughter and hid her scarlet face in her hands.

"Oh, whilikers! I didn't see anything, did you boss?" Sam coughed. "Flip that coin before darkness covers the face of the earth and we all three have to milk because no one can see to check fence."

Rick flipped the quarter, slapping it onto the back of his tanned hand. The evening sun made the hairs on his arm and hand look translucent, gold with a reddish tinge ever so slight.

"Well, just as I had hoped. Sam, you're in for the thrill of a lifetime. You've just been selected by the gods of fortune to relieve the Jersey damsels of their white gold. How'd you get so lucky?"

"I'm always lucky," Sam groaned. "How'd I ever end up in a dairy barn instead of the flats of the Southwest tending beef cattle, I'd like to know." He grinned.

"A barn full of cows doesn't exactly smell like the windswept deserts of New Mexico, you know. Course, it's not so bad, we keep a clean barn. But the thing that tears me up is that as soon as the barn cleaner shovels out the gutters and I get clean straw spread around, those bossies just mess it up all over again. You'd think they'd been born in a barn, the way they act!" With that Sam winked at Pamela who started to laugh again, saying,

"And, besides, they should have a little *respect*."

Sam's eyes rolled toward the heavens as he turned to walk to the barn.

"Come on, girl," Rick grabbed her hand, and started toward the stable to saddle up the horses. "I'm so late getting started." And in a sweet, uncomplaining little-boy voice added, "Someone wouldn't let me."

"What?" Pamela asked, "You mean that I held you back? I truly didn't mean to, I'm sorry." Rick laughed, swinging her up into his arms, kissing her soundly on the mouth.

"That should let you know how pleased I am at the delay," he nuzzled his nose delicately across the tip of her own in an Eskimo kiss. "You can impede progress any time you take a notion. Of course, it took two people to do so this time, as it probably will in the future."

She looked into his violet eyes, eating up the adoring look with which he was loving her.

"Oh, Rick!" she exclaimed as she tightened her arms around his neck, pulling his dear face into the space between her jawline and shoulder. "Oh, Rick! I love you so much. You make me the happiest I have ever been in my entire lifetime. You are like a dream, and sometimes I'm afraid that I will awaken and find you gone."

"Oh, little lady, I'm not going anyplace without you. You'll have a whole lifetime to get your fill, and I'm the lucky guy who gets to feed you portion after portion of love and attention. How I will enjoy that!"

Setting her down after carrying her over the threshold into the red stable, he took a rich chestnut brown saddle out of the tack room, carrying a Navajo saddle blanket. Quickly saddling up the Palomino, he then saddled up the Arabian in a well used and cared for saddle of identical shading as the mare. A red saddle blanket with butterscotch, deep brown and white stripes zigzagging along its edges like shafts of lightening permanently captured in the wool, was placed across the mare's back first.

"You have a striking mount there," Pamela said as Rick finished tightening the last cinch and led the horses out to the yard.

"Thank you," he smiled. "Here, let me help you up," and he gave her a boost after she placed her boot into the stirrup and started pulling herself into position to swing her right leg over the Palomino's croup.

"Thanks, Rick," she smiled down at him, then watched with pride, feeling the peculiar fluid sensation which always vied to make her short of breath whenever she watched the beauty of the man she had grown to love. That delicious sensation washed over her without warning, anytime, anyplace. Had Rick not announced *where* he first saw her, she knew that saying no to the physical and spiritual need which surfaced in the haymow, would have been impossible.

'He did ask me to marry him,' she thought quietly as she watched him swing into the sable brown saddle. 'I think!' she dizzily thought and laughed a little.

Hearing Pamela laugh, Rick smiled over at her, and started walking his horse toward the corral fence which connected with a lane leading to the green hills beyond.

"Good thing we have daylight saving time in this state," Rick observed. "We can still get four hours of work accomplished. And, it shouldn't even take that long. How does three hours of work sound to you, with one hour of sightseeing, or whatever?" Winking at her, they rode side by side to the gate. Rick dismounted, and opened the bars allowing Pamela to pass after leading his mount ahead of her. Pushing the gate shut again, he slid a wooden bar through the catch and swung back into his saddle.

"Let's go!" he exclaimed and started walking his horse sedately along a path which was fenced in by more corral on either side.

"How much riding have you done, Pamela?"

"Oh, a little bit, I guess," she answered.

"Well, we should be careful of your injuries, I would imagine. There is no hurry, and it's sort of nice just to walk the horses once in awhile. Would you like that?"

Pamela smiled. "That's fine. Maybe later on today we can try a trial run and see how it makes me feel. The only way I will know is to try it."

"O.K. Good idea," and Rick reached over to take her hand, disarmingly drawing it to his mouth to kiss her fingertips.

A thrill ran through Pamela's body as she watched him gently caressing her tiny, pink fingertips which lay over his tanned fingers. He carefully placed her hand back onto her jean-clad leg.

Coming to the end of the lane, they followed the fence which was a series of uniform posts set into the ground exactly six feet apart. Six rows of tightly stretched barbed wire, spaced two feet apart horizontally made the fencing look neat while being a practical conductor of electricity if ever an added punch other than the barbs were needed.

"The fence looks so durable. But, don't those barbs hurt the cattle?" Pamela asked.

"The cattle would feel a prick, something like when someone used to pop you with a rubber band during your school days. Same with the electricity, it just gives them a no nonsense jolt which takes the want to out of going where they shouldn't."

"It must have taken a long time to build. There are miles of fence!" Pamela exclaimed.

"Yes, we spent quite a few weeks getting this put in last fall. This ground was hard as ice since it is quite rocky in all its geological layers in the first place." He smiled, remembering aloud the rock-picking crews of high school kids whom he had to hire every spring to clear the newly exposed stones which a year of natural evolution, plus digging, and plowing always left on top of the fields.

"Anything that is exposed on top of a field is hiding just beneath the surface in the surrounding pasture lands, also," he explained.

By this time they had ridden over to the back forty, and were riding between the fence which protected a large expanse of knee-high corn from the keen appetites of the registered Angus beef cattle which roamed through the white birch and elm of the higher pasture. Red oak and prickly ash on the hilly expanses gradually flattened into marsh where tamarack pines rose majestically above the flowering yellow cup of the cowslips growing amongst peat bogs and rushes.

Redwing blackbirds perched at an angle on blades of swaying bull rushes, trilled their clear melodies to anyone who would listen.

"Oh, how I love redwing blackbirds!" Pamela exclaimed. "They were always the first heralds of spring and I remember they used to appear during the month of March on my father's farm. The first time I would see them every year would be as I walked along our driveway to catch the school bus of a morning. The air would be cold even though the snows would be mostly thawed. Thin sheets of ice would glaze the mud puddles on the driveway, and I remember hearing the birds trill as the plastic-sounding squeeze of breaking ice met the soles of my shoes." She happily looked into Rick's eyes and continued: "The air would be so fresh, and the sky so blue! What a welcome change from the whitish-grey heavens of the winter months. Yes, redwing blackbirds always make me feel happy when I hear them sing. They were always the promise of happy, free days ahead, for only one quarter remained of school before summer vacation started. Our summer vacations were of three months duration."

Rick had dismounted during her narration and started fixing a ruptured line of barbed wire. He took a strand of barbs in his hand, using the wire cutter to trim the broken end, then fastened it securely over an insulator the size of a quarter, which he had already nailed onto a pine fence post.

"Here, catch!" he called, tossing something up to Pamela who was still astride the Palomino.

She caught the flying object and examined it. It was a broken piece of what appeared to be ceramic.

"What is this?" she asked.

"That is the culprit which, when broken, lets the fence sag. It's an insulator. I had to pull it off the fence post with my pliers in order to put this new one on. Its function is to hold the wire securely in place. It also conducts electricity without interference if one needs an electric fence. See? You drape the wire through this little groove on them like so," and he traced the wire with his leather-gloved fingertip in explanation.

"How do they break?" Pamela wanted to know.

"Oh, I don't know. It could be because of several things, including a sudden, heavy pull on the wires from a cow straining against it while trying to stretch her neck under the wire to get at what appears to be greener grass on the other side of the fence, or the hooves of a deer which got caught while jumping the fence."

"Do you mean a deer can clear a fence six to eight feet high?" Pamela asked in amazement.

"Easily," Rick rejoined, "they can really jump, and these fences run across two thousand acres of deer trails which the wildlife have been using for years to get to the ponds and slough areas for morning and evening drinks."

"Is that right?" Pamela wanted to know. "What time in the mornings and evenings do they come to be refreshed?"

"Well, the actual time according to the clock varies in northern Minnesota because of the four seasons we enjoy. However, according to the sun, they come at the same time every day... dawn and dusk. So, if you are ever driving at those times in your little car, Pamela, keep one eye open for deer which are crossing the highways at that time. O.K.?" He looked up at her with concern.

"Thank you Rick, and yes, I will be careful," Pamela said as she watched Rick slide pliers and hammer into the carry-all which hung from his belt. He grasped a carpenter's bag in his gloved hand, strode to his mount and climbed on, settling with natural ease onto the back of his prized Arabian.

"Let's swing along this section of fence," he said as he took a sharp right. "Be careful of the overhanging branches of this scrub oak," he cautioned. "They can knock an unsuspecting rider right off his keester if he's not careful."

Pamela grinned and followed down the narrow trail guiding her golden horse through brush and low branches which Rick held aside for her. The mare flicked her white tail at horseflies which angrily attacked from the disturbed foliage on either side.

"Ouch!" Pam squealed.

"Did the prickly ash get you?" Rick turned around to look at her.

"Is that what this horrid shrub is? Golly, the thorn pricks sting!"

"That it does. A person really needs chaps out in this stuff. I should have put mine on you, but they are back in the tack room. I didn't really intend to take this particular trail, so I didn't bring them. But, once out here I saw that this stretch of fence doesn't look right. We don't have to go very far before we come upon a hay meadow which is cleared of the prickly ash."

"O.K.," Pamela sang out, "lead on, great and glorious leader." She rode along occasionally rubbing her smarting knee and thigh.

A mile of fencing was checked before the horses carried their riders into a clearing which was bathed in waning shafts of warm afternoon sunshine. There was a slight, welcome breeze which kept the faithful evening pests, the scourge of Minnesota, at bay – mosquitoes.

"Where's the state bird, that which seems to grow in such healthy profusion up here?" Pamela asked.

"You mean the mosquitoes?" Rick laughed. "They're not fond of breezes, so we're lucky this evening."

"Oh, look at the beautiful sight," Pamela breathed. A hayfield, sporting thick, dulling green windrows of freshly mown hay which had been raked together to dry before being made into bales, lay before them. White birch trees, red oak, and an occasional elm populated the lush woods which grew neatly around the four edges of the meadow. Red sumac and green fern mixed with wild flowers of yellow brown-eyed Susan and lavender flocks grew around the base of the trees. A few round bales weighing up to fifteen hundred pounds each, had already been put up and were lying on their sides like huge cinnamon rolls around the edges of the field where three windrows had been.

"I see that Sam managed to get up a few bales today in spite of having to drive fifty miles for parts to fix the baler."

The baler itself was parked with the green tractor in a protected spot against the far side of the field.

"I don't remember ever having seen a baler that big before! It looks like a green, one-story fan casing!" Pamela exclaimed. "Are you sure it isn't a cage for a giant squirrel? It has come complete with a giant wheel attached inside the mesh caging. What is that for?"

"The hay wraps around inside the 'wheel', as you call it. When it is fully formed, the door trips and allows the released bale to fall onto the ground."

Rick led his lady over the rolling meadow down into a perfectly secluded little hollow where a miniature pond was being enjoyed by mosquito hawks and gnats which skimmed across its top, breaking the perfectly mirrored stillness of the water by pinpricks of disturbance. Continuing to the edge of the wood, Rick dismounted, tied the reins to a tree and came over to help Pamela get down from her Palomino. Her right foot touched the prickly resistance of alfalfa stubble, and she was glad that she had her cowboy boots on which would protect her ankles from getting scratched into bleeding by the relentless blades.

Walking beside Rick, listening to the crunch their feet made as he led her across the stubble, she enumerated all the things for which she was most thankful. He and Davie topped the list.

Approaching a bale Rick untied his saddle roll and spread it on the ground adjacent in order that they have a backdrop against which to sit.

Kneeling down to dig into the saddle bag which he had carried along, Rick drew a bottle of Piesporter wine, a small loaf of French bread and a chunk of sharp cheddar cheese from its depths. Pamela sat leaning against the bale, listening to the leaves rustling, watching Rick as he arranged the food.

Rick reached across the blanket and took Pamela by the hand.

"Here, let's get some fresh hay out of a windrow and spread it over the blanket too. There are no thistles in this particular field, and that will make for a softer seat," he explained.

Twenty minutes later the French bread was gone, the remaining cheese lay in a jagged, thick lump on its cellophane wrap which was being tickled by an occasional gust, the wine bottle shone golden in the sunlight from the remaining one third of liquid in the bottom.

Rick's arm was around Pamela as they sat against the fragrant hay, cuddled and peacefully contented from the ride and food. He looked down at her, taking her lovely face in his massive hand and turned it to him. He looked deeply and long into her grey eyes. The charcoal-rimmed irises were almost one with the pupils which had dilated from the shadow cast by his body.

"Are you the little lady who is going to be my wife?" Rick tenderly asked, kissing her before she could respond.

Long, sweetly, tenderly he kissed her until she could not fight the waves of desire which became stronger and stronger in her body. She thought of how they had been brought by circumstances into each other's lives, how unlikely everything had been. She marveled, as his hands gently traced the contours of her side; at how each of them had not been drawn into liaisons with anyone else since the death of both mates. Now, finding one another had been so right, so timely.

All thoughts were swept away as she found herself being laid carefully onto the sweet-smelling hay. Rick's strong left arm was cradling her close to his firm chest, while the other lay lightly over her midriff, resting ever so lightly across her breast as he stroked her chestnut hair. Nestling his fingertips deeper into the mass atop her head, the pin became loosened, and as they kissed and rolled, curls spread across the jacket which he had laid beneath her head.

Having come to the knowledge within herself that this was the man for her, she drew her dainty hand softly between his massive shoulders, up the warmth of his neck into the silkiness of his blond hair. With gentle pressure she urged his handsome face not to leave hers, and the little kisses became long and deep, his prowess leading her into paths of blissful oblivion.

She slowly slid her arms toward herself carefully. Lovingly, her hands came to rest on each side of his handsome face, fingertips lost in his thick, silky blond curls. Raising himself above her, he pulled her more tightly into his arms, lowering his face to hers, he started kissing her lips again; softly at first, and then, all of a sudden, it was as if a tiger became unleashed in his core. Her arms went urgently around his chest, nestled beneath his strong arms. He parted her lips with deftness, and she found herself kissing and being kissed excitingly. His hand strayed to her side, and started sliding slowly over the soft mound of her clothed bodice. She had forgotten the sensations which a man's touch used to evoke, and the surge of pleasure was so intense that it made her gasp. She felt his hand pull carefully but firmly on the first snap of her cowboy shirt just above the breasts, and his lips left hers, traveling over her pretty chin down into the warm hollow of her throat. Then slowly, slowly, each kiss exquisitely tender and soft, made its way to the silky whiteness which even her bathing suit had not allowed the sun to touch.

"Oh, my darling!" he breathed, "you are even more beautiful than I had imagined."

Another snap popped open, and another. The frontal clasp of her lacy bra was impatiently opened by the capable thumb and forefinger of one callused, but gentle hand. And then, in delight, the hand gently discovered that which until this moment had been only a suggestion – a visual symphony of propriety and grace.

Pamela thought she could not stand prolonging another minute delicious and tender though it was.

"Pamela, Pamela," he whispered, "I want you." His hand finished opening her shirt. She felt strong fingers unbuckling her belt and unsnapping her Levi's. Slowly, so as not to catch her tender flesh, he unzipped the fly. She felt his hand raise from her bosom, and heard, "Oh, you poor little lamb," as he saw her scars for the first time since tending them with his brother at the hospital.

She opened her eyes and looked at him, and saw tears welling into the violet orbs which she had grown to love so well. He returned her look, and then, as if trying to make up for all the excruciating pain she had suffered a few months earlier, bent down with golden head and kissed the flaming red wounds.

Very touched by his compassion, Pamela felt a tear escape her eyes, run down the side of her temples and into her hair.

Carefully he drew himself above her. The sight of him made her suddenly feel shy. She recognized the shyness as being the exact feelings with which she had greeted the moment of loving on her wedding night. But, as on that lovely night ten years earlier, the overwhelming love and need coursing through her mind and body made the woman in her respond to the man in Rick. She reached up for him. His shirt buttons felt hard on her skin. She took her little hands, and started unfastening them. Finally succeeding, she spread the material apart, and luxuriated in the soft, yet hard touch of his skin and muscle against the soft swells of her body. She had forgotten how remarkable that particular sensation was, and felt herself swept into an absolute banquet of sensuality. Abandoning herself to it, and the spiritual oneness which they had already achieved since meeting, they rejoiced in each other over and over, again and again.

Later, she could never smell the scent of freshly mown hay without instantly being reminded of one of the most delicious moments of her life, the one which took place in the hayfield that day.

The days following Rick's proposal were filled with joy as they grew closer and closer in heart and mind. The fact that their ecstasy had already joined them as man and wife didn't bother either of them because they instinctively knew that all that was lacking was setting a date for the formalities. There was no question in their minds that they belonged and were meant to be together. They recognized that their individual experience of life had fashioned them for each other. They were truly equally yoked in every sense of the word, and had been brought together by some goodness in life which was greater than they. Both felt and knew this. They joyed in it and relaxed in their new found love, being wise enough to know that was it not right, they would not feel as they did, nor would they have been brought into each other's lives at this time. Rick never would have been at the hospital when Pamela was brought in. Time had perfected a gift for them in each other, handing it to them when their psyches were ready for it. Because of past pain, they appreciated each other, and loved with all of their hearts. They were brought together that their joy might be full, they were certain.

Chapter Five

After Pamela's introduction into Rick's arms, it seemed as if the whole world was filled with wonder. The rolling hills which were spread and designed like a patchwork quilt behind the red barns reminded her of the pictures in books she used to find in her father's library. The lanes made by the milk cows through the pastures and adjoining wooded plots provided the lovers a place to walk and talk, to love and laugh away from the four increasingly curious children. Pamela's son had so much going on with his friends at school and at church that he paid little attention to them. And although he would smile sometimes when noticing Pamela singing under her breath again, as had been her habit before his father died, Davie's sense of privacy and love of his mother would not allow him to spoil anything by prematurely guessing aloud. He wanted her to be happy and wanted to see the sadness in her cease. Their shared tragedies had deepened his instinctive understanding. He was protective of his mother and did not want to intrude on something which he felt was still a very private affair. Seeing his mom date such a nice man was a real bonus which life had brought his way too, he figured. Therefore he could not have approved more.

"Rick? Did you say we have to go find a newborn calf right this minute?" Pamela was again spending the day with Rick; enjoying the massive white, turn of the century home with its twelve foot ceilings and ornately carved woodwork. She especially loved the front verandah which proudly displayed four artistic pillars.

"Yes, Pamela. One of the springer heifers has thrown her calf during the night. She's out in the meadow feeding, but I wasn't able to spot the calf. She must have hidden it in a thicket out in the east pasture. Would you like to go along?"

"Are we going to take the horses?" Pamela excitedly queried, "and, by the way, what in the world is a springer heifer?"

Rick laughed. "A springer heifer is a cow which is about to birth her first calf; a bride, expecting for the first time, if you will. And, yes, we can take the horses if you wish, but I have so much to do I'd rather take the old beater so I can load a cord of wood on the way back to the house. It's August already and with the late spring we had this year causing tardy hay crops, I'll have to finish baling tomorrow. The hay is still damp. So, we will get wood today."

"I enjoy riding in that old red truck, Rick. It's more fun than most things I've ridden in!" Pamela laughed.

She hurriedly hung up the dish towel, let the water out of the sink, scoured it a wee bit, and squirted lotion on her hands as she made a dash for the door. Rick was standing there watching her with a pleased smile on his face. As she hastily approached and passed ahead of him to go out the door, he playfully swatted her on the derriere and grabbed her hand, pulling her backwards for a kiss. Bending her over until her head almost touched the kitchen floor, he planted one on her. Feet flying, she frantically grasped his muscular forearms, and started laughing while his mouth was still on hers. Standing her upright, he held her in his arms.

"Rick, you are such a wonderful Romeo!" she said, momentarily leaning against his chest. "Mmmmm, give me some more, kind sir," and she threw her arms around his neck and pressed eager lips to his own. His hands swept to the front of her blouse. She melted at his touch. With one strong swoop, he picked her up off the floor and carried her with steady sure strides through the house to his bedroom, kissing her with one lingering kiss all the way. Her heart beat madly like the wings of a hummingbird as she remembered two weeks ago in the hayfield.

He laid her carefully on the bed. She shut her eyes, again overwhelmed with the inborn sense of modesty with which she had always been plagued. Sensing her need for a reassuring touch, he tenderly, gently led them into passionate, healing waves of ecstasy where emotional and physical wounds of the past found solace and surcease. Two spirits became as one.

As Pamela responded, long hair cascaded from the chignon on top of her head. The golden pin loosened. It lay sparkling in the heavy tangle of thick brown curls spread over the pillows. The nape of her neck felt deliciously naked on the cool bedclothes.

"Rick, Rick, I love you," she shuddered in joy as her arms squeezed around his massive hard body as tightly as her strength would allow. "Love me. Love me. I need you," and she threw all reservations to the winds. "Oh, how I love you, if only I could express how deeply I do," and she started to love him with her body as if she had never loved before. He moaned in the pleasure she brought, drank it in as if drinking fresh water for the first time after being lost in a desert.

She raised herself above him after he rolled back onto the mattress, and in great tenderness started to trace the outline of his beautiful face, neck, chest and torso, filling her tender little hands with the goodness and beauty of the man. She memorized every little detail by touch alone, so that nothing could ever take him away from her... nothing.

'I will love you as long as you will have me,' she tenderly thought as she looked at his golden body spread before her like a feast at a banquet.

He opened his violet eyes and looked lovingly upon her, lifted her tenderly toward him and laid her upon his chest.

"You are the most beautiful thing that has ever happened to me," he whispered. "When shall we get married, Kline Traub?"

"Would you like it sooner or later?" she dreamily sighed.

"Sooner," he said as he held her for a few minutes. Then, with a sigh of resignation conformed to the mundane. "I suppose we should go find that little calf, shouldn't we?"

"Rick? Maybe we should have waited. We aren't married." She hadn't heard his question.

"In whose eyes aren't we married at this point?" Rick asked.

"I hope not God's," her voice sounded frightened.

"Perhaps the same High Priest who created and understood the passionate attraction which he caused to flower between Adam and Eve before their act of disobedience, will accept the innocence and purity of His original concept in our case also," Rick answered.

Pamela nestled more comfortably.

"Darling," he continued, "I sense that you feel remorse. Please don't. God has already given us physical love as an enjoyment and soul bonding. I offered marriage before we took committed license. We didn't prey upon each other.

It just joyfully happened today. The other day it tenderly happened."

"But I waited until marriage the first time. Of course, I didn't know full-blown passion then as I did when you came into my life," she conjectured.

"Maybe the ancient reference in I Corinthians 7, v.36 in our *Guide for Living* will help ease your mind."

"What does it say, Rick?"

"It says that if a man thinks he behaved uncomely toward his virgin..."

"I am not a virgin, Rick," Pam blushed.

Rick chuckled.

"You know that we can apply it in our case... now listen up, Kline Traub," he kissed the top of her dear head.

"Proceed, Right Reverend Jarvis!" she teased to hide her ambivalence.

"Are you going to listen or not, you minx?" He sounded determined.

"I'll listen," her eyes sparkled.

"O.K.! Where was I. Oh, yes. Back to the virgin who fell under the magic spell of her betrothed's adulation," he playfully kissed her nose. "It continues to say, 'if she pass the flower of her age, and need so require, let him do what he will, he sinneth not: let them marry.' And, darling? We honored each other with the most private, most precious gift we could bestow upon one another a few minutes ago. We gave our bodies and spirits in complete agreement and love. I pledge my fidelity to you, my soon-to-be-bride. You run through my veins it seems; I love you so dearly! And I think God's original plan between man and woman was for desire to flow purely, naturally, monogomously between them, because that is what I feel for the first time in my life and it has everything to do with you!"

"Oh, darling, how wonderful!" Pamela sat upright. "Does a wedding at the end of this month sound good to you?"

"Perfect!" he crowed, grabbing her tightly into his arms, kissing rapidly over Pam's entire face, ending with one on the tip of the little nose.

Laughing breathlessly, she wriggled out of his grasp, bounced onto the side of the bed, threw her long legs over and said jauntily, "Bet I can beat you getting dressed!" and with that she jumped up, scooped up her clothes and sprinted toward the bathroom with jean legs, shirt arms and bra straps dangling from her loaded arms.

"Here, you forgot something," he laughed.

She turned around, covering the front of herself with the armful of clothing. There stood Rick holding a delicate pair of bikinis between his massive forefinger and thumb, dangling them like a white flag.

"Throw them to me," she commanded, blushing shades of purple.

"Come and get them," he laughed.

She charged the length of the dining room through which she had just scampered reaching out for the article. Laughing, he hid them behind his back just as she took hold, which drew her arm behind him and thrust her off balance, causing their naked chests to meet.

"Mmmm, you feel so good," he said, moving against her silkiness.

"Rick, stop it. If you want me to go help find that calf instead of landing in the bed again, stop it!" and he gave her a quick kiss, deposited the article in question on top of the rest of the clothes which by this time were on the floor between their naked feet, and went back into the bedroom to get dressed. After a quick shower and having twisted her hair into a burnished knot, tendrils escaping around her face and forehead, Pam came out of the bathroom, hurried to check the bed to see whether or not he had remade it and out of the door they went.

"Want to try driving the old beater?" he asked.

"Sure, why not," she laughed.

"O.K. then. Hop up here." He said as he opened the big door and lifted her by the belt hoops onto the running board. "That's a pretty big step!" he exclaimed.

"Yes, especially when my legs are feeling like water after the delicious exercise we just had," she whispered into his ear which was suddenly on the some level as her mouth. She nipped his earlobe playfully.

"Ouch, you little rascal!" and he cupped one big hand and softly swatted her sitter-downer. She jumped up onto the seat in a burst of laughter.

"How do you get this thing started?"

"Well, you go out and crank it." Rick said as she laughed again. "Actually, you don't have to crank it. You start it like this," and he reached in across her, purposely rubbing his tan arm against her lovely chest.

"Now, you stop that, you hear?" and Pam tried to concentrate on what he was showing her. Getting it started, he crossed over in front of the red cab and climbed into the other side.

"Hang on," she laughed us she stomped on the clutch and brake, grinding the stick into reverse. "Do you always park it nose first against the granary on a downgrade?" she teased.

"No, I just thought it would be good practice for you!" he exclaimed.

"Well, I'm afraid that the pretty new paint job on this building is going to have a tortured wood effect ingrained soon, unless you don't mind if I rev the motor to a dull roar in my efforts to get going backwards. Otherwise I will roll right into the side of it when I release this stiff clutch!"

"Go ahead, nothing can hurt this baby!" he insisted patting the dash. "Just don't knock the granary down. I don't have time to build a new one before the honeymoon."

She pushed on the footfeed, bent down and wedged a little pencil against it to keep it humming after putting the stick back into neutral. Then she pushed one foot against the brake where it joined proximity to the other which was depressing the clutch. Engine roaring, feet pushing with all the strength she could muster to keep the pedals depressed, she again ground it into reverse.

"Why don't you grind me a pound, too?" Rick teased.

"Oh, that's bad," she grimaced at him. "Hang on!" and the truck gave a mighty leap backwards. The spinning tires threw grass and dirt in all directions and filled the cab with dust and fuzz. Choking and laughing, she finally kicked the pencil out of the way with her boot, and guided the dump truck carefully backwards, using the side-mirror to gauge the distance between it and the pumphouse.

"Not bad, little woman," he patted her leg. "Let's go down this lane. I'll open the fences as we come to them."

Pamela nosed the truck down the road, marveling at the rich, black dirt called loam which was peculiar to this part of her native Minnesota. It was a sharp contrast to the sage-colored soil in southern Arizona where she had spent the last twelve years of her life. She also marveled how two different types of soil could produce the same beautiful crops of hay and grain. True, on her friend's ranch in Arizona, additives had to be carefully worked into the soil, and irrigation was an absolute essential. Different hybrid seeds were used, but the results were the same.

'Can't raise cotton up here, though,' she observed... 'too cold.' As they bounced along in the truck the green cornstalk leaves undulating in the breeze made her appreciate the beauty of all things natural. Nutty, deep scents of loam exalted with the sweetness of sun-kissed verdure, whispering summertime.

"Rick, look how the afternoon sunshine bathes the crest of that hill in *golden* light. This morning it was bathed in pure *white* sunshine. I like this four o'clock glow better, I think. It makes the shadows from the oak trees along the edge of the hill look more mysterious, and the grass look a deeper green, don't you think?"

Rick followed her gaze to the knoll. His golden brown Jersey cows were grazing peacefully against the scene she had described. "Yes, it is pretty at this time of day. And I like early morning just as well," he observed. "At that time of day, it seems as if the whole world has been freshly bathed in sparkling dew, and it smells so fresh and clear."

"You love the ranch, don't you," Pamela softly concluded.

"Yes, I do. I don't think I could ever be happy being cooped up permanently in a city, magnificent though it may be." He smiled over at her and covered her hand on the steering wheel momentarily. All of a sudden in hushed tones he asked, "Could you be happy living on a ranch?"

She looked at him. Then, looking away to concentrate on the farm road down which she was guiding the lumbering truck, she asked, "Do you mean constantly? If so, I don't know. Although I yearn for nature and its beauty, I also like the city and the cultural things it affords. But, I have tried both and I must say that I need both. When I live in the city and can't afford to escape to the country on the weekends, I feel trapped. But, when living in the country, if I can't visit the city to shop or browse through museums, go to the symphony or whatever, I feel starved inside. I need both to round out my life."

"That's perfect! I share your sentiments exactly." He looked across the cab at her, "I can't get over how well we are suited to one another in every way. And, as we grow to know one another more, we find we are more compatible than we had thought in the first place. I can't imagine us ever having an argument, can you?"

"That depends upon what you want to argue about," Pamela laughed.

"Let's try for our first. Have you pinpointed an exact date in August which would seem to be an appropriate wedding day?" he smiled at her again.

"How about the sixth Thursday of this month?"

Rick shook his head. "Seriously madam, when are you going to take my hand and join me in wedded bliss?"

"Well, I wish it could be before school starts in order to get Davie settled. Then perhaps we could intrigue one of his favorite aunts into coming to live at the house with the other children while we honeymoon, or tend to matters out of state. I do have to inform Mr. Randolph you know, even though I *am* so elated over the prospect of living with you, I feel unduly sad that we won't be living in Arizona... which means that I will have to give up my career. I love my work, Rick," she looked imploringly at him.

"Who said anything about giving up your interests, sweetheart?"

"No one, but I just assumed..."

"Well, little darling, all that meets the eye isn't necessarily what you are getting, unless you prefer it that way."

"What do you mean, Rick?"

"I mean, whoa! Watch it, sweetheart!"

Pamela again turned to look where she was going, slamming on the brakes as she never intended to get so close to the fence gate which loomed a few feet from the nose of the truck.

"First fence," she sang out as she braked the two-ton beast to a halt. "I've stopped this two-ton wonder, and now you may proceed to usher us into that fairyland of green carpet and draperies, dear sir," she cheerfully announced.

"Yes? This is a wonder, all right," Rick patted the dash and laughed. "One wonders how long it will keep running, it is so old."

Reaching the edge of the woods, she stopped the engine, shifted into first, and tried to open the massive door. Rick came around to her side and yanked it open, reached up and lifted her down against himself, holding her there for one, delicious moment. Kissing her long and hard, he put her down, and keeping his arm protectively around her, walked a few yards across the clearing into the woods. Pretty soon the path became very narrow, since it was used only by cattle, and they had to walk single file.

"Roll down your sleeves to protect your skin from thistles and prickly ash," he reminded her.

Doing as she was told, and putting on an extra pair of leather gloves which Rick had brought along, she again forged ahead behind her slim-hipped partner.

"Let's cut through here. There's a pretty little deer path I want to show you," Rick said as he stood aside, parting the boughs of trees under which they were to pass.

"Where is the deer path?" she asked.

"Here, dear. Do you see it?" and he pointed a foot beyond the toes of her cowboy boots to the tender blades of grass which had been gingerly pressed down by something light of foot. "They use this short cut to go to the pond. Sometime we will have to come and sit in the tree stand and watch them," he said as he pointed to the loft platform which had been built up in the tree above their heads.

"Oh, I didn't see that," she exclaimed.

"We use it for hunting during deer season."

Her face fell as she looked at him in surprise.

"The poor deer," she sighed. "I can't understand how anyone could shoot anything so beautiful. They are so harmless."

"They are, but their numbers have to be controlled in order that disease or starvation don't destroy them. The herds are controlled by the state, which in so doing protects them. It is better to allow people to hunt and provide their families with good meat than to let it go to waste, or the herds to become overpopulated and starve to death."

"I see your logic, and of course, that is the only humane thing to do, isn't it," she thoughtfully conjectured. "But, ever since I almost died in that accident, life seems so precious to me whether it is mine, or any other living creature's. I can't bear to see a life needlessly taken;" and she followed down the path behind him. Dropping sharply to the bottom of a hill they reached a slough full of cattails and reeds. A duck flew quacking out of a nest hidden in the rushes.

They stood and watched the mother duck calling and scolding her ducklings who were swimming in a queue of pairs on the surface of the still pond. The bigger bird flapped at them with her wings, hurrying ahead in the water to hide them in the rushes. One by one they glided out of sight, some spinning around like fuzzy little tops before zeroing in on home. She and Rick heard a few more rustlings and clucking sounds as matronly instincts guided the ducklings under a downy breast in an effort to hide the tiny treasures from a presumed enemy. Running forward as quietly as they could, Rick and Pamela dropped on their knees into the wet grass on the edge of the shoreline. Peeking carefully through reeds parted by Rick's hand, Pamela could see the nest where the mother duck was sitting quietly, looking like a decoy for all one could tell. Suddenly Pamela giggled, for out from under the left wing a fuzzy little head popped. It was met with a quick peck applied by an agitated mother to her disobedient duckling's head. The little one lost no time in pulling back into downy safety.

"Look Pamela. Look. There is something brown in the rushes on the far side. Oh, no. I think it's the calf we are looking for. I hope he hasn't drowned," and Rick scrambled to his feet, pulling her up with him. They dashed around the end of the slough and there was the newborn calf, colored as beautifully as its mother.

"Is it still alive, Rick?"

Already his muscular hands were examining the calf's little nose to see whether the placenta has been licked from its nostrils to enable breath.

"Well, I'll be jiggered! Yes, the little tike is breathing. Thank God his nose was above water. Here, take my jean jacket and spread it on the grass. I'll wrap the poor little fellow in it and we'll carry him home where we can introduce him to his mother. I've got to herd his mom home and into the barn so's I can milk her to provide the calf with the first lactations. After that, we'll feed the little one calf-starter from a nippled pail, and will milk the mother morning and night with the rest of the herd." Rick looked at Pam who was spreading the jacket as he had requested. She helped him lay the wet calf within its folds.

"Here, let's tie the sleeves together over the opening to keep it closed," she said and proceeded to enforce her suggestion. Sitting back on his haunches, Rick studied her deft movements and totally absorbed face as she worked over the animal.

'Any rancher would be proud to have her for a wife,' he thought silently. 'She jumps right in and knows what to do.'

Pamela, squatting next to the calf opposite Rick, drew her attention away from Rick and looked at the calf again. Automatically, both reached to pick up the little burden at the same time. Their hands touched, causing them to look up into each other's eyes. Having seen her beautifully manicured fingernails as she pulled the leather gloves off so as to be able to assist with more dexterity, Rick thought of the cultured, smooth side of her which was so evident in the way in which she carried her body when walking, or the manner of her speech and thought process. He had never met anyone like her before who was a perfect combination of country and culture in the old tradition. He loved her. Loved her desperately.

"Come on, darling," he said as he helped her up and led the way along the path they had walked earlier. She watched his back muscles ripple under the V of his cowboy shirt as he carried the calf in his arms.

Arriving at the barn with their new little charge, Rick wondered aloud as to where Sam might be.

"Here comes Sam now, Rick," she said as her attention was drawn to the front of the barn where the hired man had just entered the door.

"Hey Sam!" Rick called, "Any messages while we were out on the back forty?"

"Yes, boss," said Sam, sprinting up into the haymow to toss down enough small oblong bales for the night feeding. "I'll give you the message when you get back. O.K?"

Rick agreed. Looking at Pamela he asked if she would like to accompany him to go cut the calf's mother out of the herd in the pasture.

"Oh yes! I'd love to go with you," she responded.

Riding out to the east pasture on Rick's quarter horse, Pamela felt a sense of exhilaration. She looked over at her fiancé who was riding masterfully beside her.

"There she is," Rick announced, "let's see if we can cut her out of the herd," and with a gentle touch of the reins against his horse's neck, the mare galloped off across the clipped grass. Pamela galloped beside him until Rick signaled, indicating that she should skirt away far enough to wedge between the desired cow and the beef steers who were hosting her in their pasture. Pamela thrilled to the task, loving the feel of the air as it surged against her face and body. The combined feelings of power emanating from the horse, and of togetherness pouring from Rick's mind to hers as he guided her into being the other half of him gave a wonderful sense of well-being, worth and belonging.

"That gal is as good on a horse as I!" Rick surged with pride as he watched her weaving in and out of the brush, rock, and cattle. Finally the new mother was brought at a trot away from the herd, and guided to the lane which was corralled on both sides.

When they got back to the barn, Pamela excused herself to go into the house where the children were waiting, having walked home from day camp where they'd been receiving swimming instructions.

Rick, in the meantime, walked into the barn where Sam helped him drive the freshened bovine into a stantion. Together they secured a chain around her neck, and marked a placard with her name and the date before sliding it into the appropriate slot nailed to the partition above her head. Then they carried the newborn calf to lay him before the mother on a fresh bed of straw. The mother started sniffing her calf, gingerly lolling her long tongue out to see if indeed this was the upstart who had interrupted her day. Being satisfied that indeed it was, she lent herself to the task of cleaning him.

"A little late in cleaning your calf, aren't you girl?" Sam questioned. "But now that you have accepted him, we'll bring him alongside you where he can find the source of the good stuff!" and he and Rick grabbed hold, carrying the calf to its mother's side.

The calf called softly to its mother, she turned her head around to see that the little one was O.K., licking him again. The calf put two wobbly, spindly legs ahead of its head, planting his little cloven feet onto the cement floor. Shakily raising its hind quarters, he slipped and slid around, tiny hooves flying everywhere, until with a terrific effort, he gingerly hoisted himself onto all fours.

"Bwaaaa!" he bawled as if outraged at the indignities of life. Rick and Sam laughed and the calf gave them a startled glance, then turned his wobbly head to face his mother's flank, banged into her gently which again knocked him onto his little front knees. Quickly scrambling up again he instinctively pooched his front legs into a V which dropped him into position to nuzzle under his mom's belly. Finally, he scored. Loud, greedy sucking noises ensued as milk dripped out of the side of his mouth onto the barn floor.

All of a sudden he sneezed. Milk flew everywhere, as Sam and Rick again laughed.

"You greedy little boy, take your time and you won't choke!" Rick said. "By the way, Sam. What was the message which came while I was out on the back forty? Maybe my disappointment in this calf not being a future producer of at least seventeen thousand pounds of milk annually will be assuaged by what you've been told regarding Don and Sis. Then I won't miss the two thousand, two hundred and eighty-eight dollars minus the cost of feed this little bugger would have, as a gal, brought into our coffers every year. Well, I guess in the long run, he will pay off as sire to genetically sound milkers. Genetics, management and type of feed are the secrets of our state of Minnesota's average fourteen thousand pounds of milk annually, per cow, you know!"

"Yeh, boss," Sam scratched his head and smiled. "As to the telephone call, you won't be disappointed as with this calf. It was the State Department calling to let you know that they have located your twin and sister-in-law. But, I couldn't relate this to you in front of Pamela as they stressed that this is to be kept in the strictest confidence. Being that you and I are assisting with the rescue operation, we're going to have to follow instructions and fly out of here as soon as they give the word. The sad part about it is that you can't tell Pamela. Once they call again, we are just going to have to get to your Lear, and jet off to Washington where we will receive further instructions."

"Oh, brother! I can't do that to Pamela, walk out without a word of explanation three weeks before our marriage!"

"Do you ever want to see your brother alive again, pal?" Sam sympathetically asked.

"You know that I do," Rick sadly answered.

"Well then, I guess that leaves you no choice," and Sam put a compassionate arm around his dearest friend who had saved him years before on yet another mission.

By the time the men were finished with the evening milking, Pamela had a dinner of chicken, mashed potatoes, gravy, several vegetables, salad, pickles, and fresh baking powder biscuits smothered in sweet butter and honey ready for the table. The five children, Sam, Rick, and Pamela made quite a table-full as they all enjoyed her country cooking.

"Where did you learn to make chicken like this?" Sam asked. "It's succulent!"

"Grandma taught my mother, and she taught me," Pamela smiled. "Thank you, all compliments gratefully received and acknowledged."

After dinner Pamela started to do the dishes, but Rick's nephews insisted that she leave that job to them.

"Whoever cooks gets out of doing dishes in this house!" they announced. That suited Pamela fine, and taking leave of the group, Pamela and Davie left for her father's home on the other side of the village.

Chapter Six

Driving up the driveway to her father's homestead, Pamela noticed an extra car sitting under the elm where she usually parked her little bug.

"I wonder whose Cadillac that is," she mused.

"Come on, Davie. Let's go in and get cleaned up. I'm ready to hit the sack. What do you say?"

"Sounds good, Mom. Pitching silage sure can wear a guy out, especially after swimming lessons."

"Last one to the house is a donkey!" Pamela sang out and with two shrieks of excitement they both took off running as fast as they could toward the house. As Davie sprinted past her, she lunged for his flying shirt tail, caught it and held him back trying to overtake the lead.

"Let go! Let go!" he laughed, and all of a sudden they both went down in a heap. Trying to crawl away, Davie wrestled with his laughing mom who was tickling the daylights out of him in an effort to render him quite helpless so she could get up and finish the race to the door which was four feet away.

"No fair, Mom!" and he started pinning her arms down.

They were laughing so hard that neither noticed the door opening, nor the dark-headed man who came to stand in the moonlight. His ring glistened like ice in its silvery glow as he smoothed his mustache.

The glint of light caught David's eye, and he looked up.

"Ned! Ned!" he cried excitedly, jumping up from his mother who law sprawled on her back in the grass.

"Hi, sport!" Ned laughed as he caught the excited boy in his arms and swung him around. With a few long strides, the darkly handsome man approached Pamela who still lay stunned in the moonlight. She saw the rich brown leather of his Italian shoes, and the cuffs of his expensive silk slacks. Looking up she felt her gaze caught by flashing black eyes above sparkling white teeth which were exposed from the exultant smile on Ned's face. Davie stood beside him, his little hand being held in Ned's firm and friendly grasp.

"Where is Jill?" Pamela asked tensely.

"Jill didn't come along this time. She wanted to, but had to go on a buying trip to New York to see next year's spring fashion displays. She must keep her shop competitive, you know."

"Davie dear. Would you gather up these jackets and my purse, and take them inside? If you'll take your bath right quick, I'll be able to take mine in ten minutes, O.K.?"

"O.K., if you promise I may sit and talk with Ned for awhile before I have to go to bed."

"You have it!" and with a sigh, Pamela sat up and brushed the grass out of her hair.

"Why don't you sit on the ground and let your feet hang over?" she dryly asked Ned. "Or will your precious pants get stained with grass?"

"Cut the sarcasm, it isn't like you, nor is it becoming," Ned said as he reached down to lift her to her feet. "Why don't we go for a walk in the moonlight instead?" he suggested.

"Ned. I am tired and smell like a barn, and I don't think it is a good idea at all for me to go for a walk with you. In fact, it isn't even a good idea for you to be here in the first place. Why *are* you here?" she demanded, suddenly angry.

He pulled her close. "You know why I am here."

"Ned. Ned, for Pete's sake! I thought we went through all of this two months ago when I left Phoenix," and in spite of herself, tears welled into her flashing eyes.

Suddenly, he was kissing her, savagely cutting off the rest of the volley of words which were exploding from her frustration.

She tried to pull away, but his arms were too strong for her and he pressed himself against her, his passion soaring.

"Oh, my love, I have longed for the sight of you, for the touch of you ever since the day I first saw you. I have vowed over and over that someday, somehow you would be mine. I will not let you go!"

The still tender incision in her midriff started knitting with little jabs of inner pain as she struggled, causing her to catch her breath and be still. Ned took it as a sign of submission.

Placing his hand in her hair, he found the golden pin which he remembered she had always worn in the chignon and pulled. Her hair came tumbling down in a burnished, silky mass over his bare arm.

Pulling her head back with his fingers which were entangled in the softness next to her warm head, he leaned over and kissed her long and hard, melting into tenderness when he heard her stifled sob. He pulled his head away, and quick as a flash she whipped one arm free and slapped him across the face, trying with her other arm to wrench herself out of his grasp.

Softly laughing, and with no effort at all, he subdued her. Holding her arms down in a bear hug, he said, "O.K.

Have it your way. I came here to reason with you, not to fight you, Pamela."

Angrily she retorted, "I don't see why you came all the way to Minnesota at all! Aren't you still engaged to Jill?"

"No."

Her heart lurched, thinking she was truly in danger of never disentangling herself. Longingly, thoughts of Rick raced through her mind, and she felt herself wishing for his protective presence.

Ned again laughed, noticing the startled look on her face. Mockingly he came within a whisper's breath from her face, and said, "We are married."

"You scoundrel! You cheap, no good hunk of flesh! Then, *why* in heaven's name are you standing here, forcing your attentions on me!"

Soothingly he said, "Because my dear, I knew that I could never get you to go with me to Jill to tell her that we were in love; I wanted to be free."

"We are *not* in love," she hissed.

"And, there was some doubt in my mind that indeed, I may never possess you as my wife; you were so adamantly the martyr in this triangle which absolutely infuriates me and makes no sense whatsoever!" He grabbed her roughly by the shoulders, "And make no mistake about it, I am going to have you one way or the other. If I can't have you for my wife, which you have said I cannot, I shall have you as my mistress!"

Pamela gasped, "You, you uncouth monster!"

"Shut your mouth!" he angrily ordered, his fury aroused, "Let me finish, Miss Goody Two Shoes. I didn't fly twelve hundred miles just to hear your side of the story. You have always pushed me away even when I knew you were wishing that you were Jill instead of yourself. Don't deny it, Pamela,"

She looked stonily at him. What he was saying was the truth, although when it had happened, she hadn't been able to explain it even to herself. But, she thought, no matter how she cut it, it had not felt like the same pure, wholesome thing which she and Rick shared even when Ned had proposed giving up Jill. The togetherness and sense of being each other's equal; a part of each other's very soul, was not there. It never had been, and she knew that it never would be. Suddenly, she understood herself.

"Ned, yes, I won't deny it. But, please try to understand that you represented a means of support, and a good life for Davie. Can't you see that we have two different sets of values morally? Nothing between us could ever be right because of Jill's love for you, and my lack of love... lust is not love. Anyone can arouse a lonely person's base feelings if they meet the lonely one's criteria regarding the opposite sex. True love needs eros *and* agape!"

"Criteria in what respect?" he asked.

"In whatever area is most important to a person. Other virtues can be lacking, but if one of great importance is met, other shortcomings can be overlooked. But, one fact cannot be overlooked, and that is the fact that you are Jill's husband. End of subject."

"In my family, it is right to have the woman you love as mistress after marrying another for position or money, or both," he enticed with a silken tongue. "I will enrich you menially as well as spiritually. I will educate your son in the finest institutions, starting right now. Whatever you choose, I will give you, darling."

She looked up at Ned. He had hit her most vulnerable spot... her son. Having been left penniless upon her husband's death other than the pittance she received from the government for their care, she had little prospect of seeing her son attend the college she had dreamed of during her pregnancy. She and her husband had worked hard to make a good education for their son available some day. Now, slowly but surely, those savings were being depleted.

The future if she married Rick? 'Obviously,' she murmured, 'he isn't able to send my son, plus his brother's children through college if disaster strikes.'

Ned's gaze was as steady and intense as a laser beam. It was as if he were reading every thought proceeding through her mind. But, that was nothing new, somehow he had always been able to tell what she was thinking, and it irritated her.

"Remember," he persuasively said, "if you say no to me, you will be depriving your son of being top-drawer in this life."

Guilt fell like a heavy mantle in her soul. Trying to free herself of it, she cried, "But what about me? Don't my feelings count for anything? Do I have to sacrifice decency for my child? I don't believe in that! If I can't respect myself, how can my son respect me? I want to be a good example. You are preposterous, Ned. Please, go away and leave me alone."

He laughed. "But you can respect yourself. Many worthwhile people have such arrangements as I've suggested. Come, darling... the world consists of more than rural, mid-western American standards."

"How dare you laugh at me!" she cast a despicable look at him. Her contempt knew no limits regarding him at that moment.

Reading her feelings, he said, "Don't rile my anger, princess. Let's go for that walk across the lawn... see it bathed in silver from the summer moon?"

"I must see Davie to bed," she strode off haughtily toward the service porch.

"Ah, yes. I forgot the little man. Pardon me." And as an afterthought, "Don't think you have gotten off easily. I intend to speak with you about this matter again, including the cowboy who seems to be gaining far too much importance in your life."

Pamela gasped, and spun on her heel to confront him.

"What cowboy?" she demanded to know.

"Come, come, Pamela," he laughed, "don't pretend you don't know of whom I speak. Why don't *you* tell me?"

"I wouldn't discuss my dog with you, sir," she concluded contemptuously.

Beyond Ned's glossy mane of pampered, styled, blow-dried hair which Pamela despised, she could see Davie waiting at the table through the dining room windows.

"What I want to know, I make it my business to find out," he breathed. "Have you never noticed a car which has been parked at the end of your father's driveway late nights on your return from the farmboy's arms? As a matter of fact, one of the gentlemen in the vehicle told me that you stopped one morning at two asking if they were lost or needed help."

"Who were they?" she whispered angrily.

"I, my dear, have had you watched ever since you left me. I told you that you would come back to me some day, and I fully intend that those words come true."

"Now you spy on me, and try to run my life! Well, Mr. DeSilva, I will not stand for it. Do you hear me?" and she fairly shouted at him in rage. "Stay out of my life. And regarding the man or men in my life," her voice dropped to a menacing whisper, "don't touch."

Grabbing her roughly by the arm, he pulled her so close she could distinguish the fine lines between his heavy, black brows.

"I, my little butterfly, do not take threats from anyone. Not my brothers, not my sisters, not my friends, not anyone... not even you. It infuriates me." Like a panther, he watched her defiant face.

"God, you are beautiful when you are angry," and she found herself being swept off the ground into his arms, her lips being crushed and bruised by his until she tasted blood. Suddenly he held her in his outstretched arms, admiring her beauty, the consternation in her face. Her eyes were closed.

Pamela felt so confused. 'If I had really believed that the things money can buy were the most important values for my son, I would have accepted Ned's offer.' She started weeping quietly in Ned's arms, too confused and tired to pull away. 'Have I made a mistake where Davie's future is concerned?' she agonized within herself. 'With an offer such as this which Ned has given tonight, I would be crazy not to accept after all is said and done. But I love Rick, even if he is poor.'

"Why do you cry, princess?" Ned softly asked.

"Oh, I am just weary. Please put me down. If you will put me down, I promise that I will carefully consider your proposal. But in return, you must promise me that you will call off the dogs. I don't think it is fair that my every movement be under observation. Please, Ned."

"Because I love you I will 'call off the dogs' as you say. All right?"

"Yes, thank you," and she gave him a grateful look as he put her feet to the ground. The grass was wet with dew, emitting a scent of sweet vegetation. Balm-of-Gilead trees from the nearby lowlands were wafting their delicious perfume through the air on gentle night breezes. She heard a nesting bird give a little peep in its sleep. Yes, she had much to think over tonight. Her son's future was at stake. And being physically disabled to a degree meant that she could not lightly discard this golden opportunity where Davie was concerned. No matter what she had to do to secure his future, it was her duty to do it. She wanted *passionately* to give him every good thing. He was the breath which gave life to her days.

'But to go against all the moral values which I have held most dear since childhood to become a kept woman? Is it worth selling myself?' Walking toward the house, her steps became heavy.

She glanced sideways at the handsome, dark man walking into the house beside her. The thought of making love to him instead of with Rick crossed her mind ever so briefly, making her feel sick in the pit of her stomach. Scrubbing the idea from her mind, Pamela noticed her son waiting at the table for the promised talk with Ned.

Wearily excusing herself, Pamela trudged up the stairs anticipating a bath and the clean bed which awaited her. Anything to escape. Sleep... sleep.

★

Ned disappeared as quickly and unexpectedly as he had come. When she came down for breakfast the next morning, she was surprised to see that he was gone. The strange car had vanished. Relieved, she went about preparing to go over her ledger.

'I must see if I have enough money to stay here the rest of this month... can you believe?' It saddened her to think that maybe she couldn't stay with Rick until the proposed marriage after all. After checking, she realized that yes indeed, the days would be few before she would be forced to go back to work. 'I knew I shouldn't have accepted my summer checks all in one sum. It's just difficult for me to make it stretch, I guess.' She wondered how she was ever going to be able to leave the cowboy whom she had grown to love so well.

The telephone rang.

"Why, Mr. Randolph! How wonderful to hear from you. I didn't expect you to get back from Europe so soon."

"Well, Pamela, I arrived home two days ago. Tell me, what good news do you have for me? I am almost afraid to ask for fear that I am being unduly hopeful that I will be seeing your face at my office door soon."

"I do have a bit of good news," Pamela responded. "The doctor said that I could return to work providing I go at it only five hours a day for awhile. I'm just not supposed to drive myself as hard as I used to presently."

"Well, that is good news. I think you will enjoy helping me sort and catalog the paintings and other artifacts which I brought home with me. There are some real beauties."

He continued with other things and then asked a hopeful, "Does that indicate what I have been anticipating – that you will be returning to your drawing board soon?"

"If by soon you mean three or four weeks, perhaps. But! I have some news which is even better, Mr. Randolph. I am getting married!"

There was silence on the other end of the telephone for a few seconds.

"Mr. Randolph, are you still there?"

"I am still here, and although I am happy because of your joy, I am disturbed and disheartened wondering if that means you will be terminating your employment with this firm. I don't want to lose you and had not even anticipated such a thing. You will be returning, will you not?"

"Oh, yes. I am sure that Rick will allow me to return and do things in an orderly fashion, if indeed I must quit. But, the other day he hinted at the possibility of me not having to give up my career. Exactly what he meant by that, I don't know at this point, but I will speak with him about it and let you know as soon as possible."

"When do you plan to tie the knot, Pamela?"

Laughing at his choice of words she told him that the formalities would hopefully be taken care of in three weeks time.

"And of course you are welcome to come throw rice at us if you wish. On second thought, you may not be able to find us because we haven't decided whether or not to have a garden affair, or to simply run off to South Dakota where one can get a license and be married all in the same day. Being it is a second wedding for me, I might prefer the latter. However, I do want Rick to experience his preference. It's a first for him," she added.

"Well, dear girl, whatever you choose, I hope that it will be a happy occasion, and that you will be coming back to the Phoenix area to live in wedded bliss. I suspect that you may be doing just that, coming here to reside."

"How strange that you project that idea. Not that I mind, for I hope that very thing myself. However, it seems such an unlikely dream. Rick loves to farm even though he is also a doctor and used to practice at Doctor's Hospital in Phoenix with his brother. But with his land being located up here, I hardly expect him to leave it behind."

"Sometimes things aren't as they seem," Mr. Randolph said.

"How strange that you should say that. Rick said the very same words a couple of weeks ago when we were discussing this subject. Do you both know something which I don't?"

Instead of answering her question, Mr. Randolph skillfully changed the subject, and said a goodbye full of fond wishes.

Slowly hanging up the receiver, Pamela pondered the coincidence of both men saying the same thing. Going to the mirror to check her appearance, she grabbed her purse and called Davie to come with her. They walked out to her little bug and started out for Rick's house, dropping Davie off at day camp en route.

Slowly driving down the gravel road which connected the highway with Rick's acres, she gazed lovingly over the green hills on which the Angus beef cattle were grazing. She looked across the road to the other side where the Jerseys were peacefully feeding, their udders freshly depleted from the early morning milking. She saw a green tractor with a mower attached which was cutting alfalfa, the hay falling down as rapidly and neatly as a row of dominoes. She wondered if it were Sam or Rick.

'I will have to tell Rick about Mr. Randolph's call and ask if I should go down to Phoenix in a few days to wrap things up there. It's the only decent thing to do unless,' she hesitated, 'I accept Ned's proposal.' But just thinking of the latter made her feel wretched merely entertaining the thoughts of breaking up with Rick. 'I will go to Phoenix just until our wedding is due. I've made up my mind, it is Rick with whom Davie and I belong. I'll tell Rick that I must go for just a few days. He will understand.'

Pulling her car into the parking lot, she jumped out and walked over to the white fence. Climbing onto the top rail, she perched herself where she could enjoy the breeze which molded her white shirt against her figure. She watched the Palomino which she had grown fond of riding.

"Here girl," she called, and the horse came trotting over to her new mistress. Nuzzling Pamela's pocket with her soft nose, the horse almost toppled her off the fence. The young woman threw her arms around the horse's neck and gave her a big hug.

"You looking for some sugar, Sugar?" she cooed. "Here, don't be so impatient. Here's some sugar for you, my caramel-colored sugar lump."

"Do I get some sugar too?" a deep voice laughed at her elbow, and she felt herself being encircled by familiar arms.

"Rick!"

"Hi, darlin'! I've been waiting for you all morning. Where've you been, beautiful?" he smiled up at her, his faultless teeth shining in the morning sunshine. Seeing him piqued Pamela's keen awareness that she might have to leave everything she had grown to love.

Rick caught her perturbed look. She went down to receive the kiss his eyes and lips were offering. She felt herself being gently pulled off the fence into his arms.

"I love you, girl," he softly whispered.

'Oh, tell me more,' she thought heartbrokenly to herself, clinging to his neck which felt warm and safe against her cheek. Feeling his strong arms around her, his hands pressed into the small of her back which brought her slenderness to him in a delicious vice of strength. She felt herself being set on fire, slowly, insistently as his warm lips closed over hers, their velvety texture responding to the soft invitation of her own. Liquid sensations attacked her abdomen and dizziness overwhelmed her. The smell of clean leather and sage overwhelmed her with desire.

'I can't leave him. I can't leave him,' she wretchedly agonized within. 'Money and prestige or no, I can't leave him!'

Feeling him stir, she heard Rick huskily say, "Come on, baby, let's go finish the fencing we had to leave the other day while we're still able."

She pushed a shock of silky hair from her flawless forehead. The burnished glow of her locks glistened in the sun as if she wore a crown. Rick wanted to reach out and touch her little white hands, run his own into the upsweep of her hair, and gently loosen the golden pin which held it fast on the crown of her head, but he controlled himself. Their eyes met.

"Come along, darling," he softly said as he took her to the stables.

In the stable Rick went to his mare while Pamela hoisted her favorite saddle off the wooden rest. She enjoyed the brown leather trimmed in silver, and often had wondered how such an obviously poor man (comparatively speaking in relation to Ned and Mr. Randolph) such as Rick could afford such a whimsical thing. There was even turquoise set into the silver. It was a magnificent piece of handiwork.

'No one from around these northern parts tooled this gorgeous thing,' she thought as she straightened the wool blanket on the mare's back before settling the cumbersome load onto the horse. 'I wonder where he got it?' She looked over the mare's back at Rick who was putting the final touches to his mount's brown trappings. Bending to work on the cinches, Pamela pulled, patting the mare's tummy.

"Come on, girl," Pamela tugged and tightened. "Why does this horse always puff up her stomach for me, Rick?" she laughed. "She never does it for you."

Striding with easy grace, boots sounding feisty on the floor, Rick came to her side. Taking the cinch from Pamela's hand, he bent down, "Here, let me give you a hand."

Patting the mare's side, he coaxed, "Come on, girly – exhale!"

The horse, seeming to understand, looked at him sideways with her big brown eyes and with a playful nip at the brim of Rick's hat, whinnied.

"Hey! Stop that, you stinker." Rick laughed and swatted her rump.

"Leave my Stetson alone, you low-life. Bite me and I'll bite you right back!"

Pamela stood watching them. 'I bet that mare loves him as much as I do, and she's jealous because she's a horse and I'm a human being.' The thought made her laugh.

"What's so funny?" Rick asked.

"Oh, I just figured out why the mare always gives me a hard time when I'm trying to saddle up. She wants you to do it. We both love you, but after all, she found you first."

Rick laughed and helped her mount. Swinging onto his own horse, he called, "Let's go," and raced ahead of her across the yards toward the green hills. With a cry of exhilaration, Pamela came charging behind him, pressing the Palomino for all she was worth. Starting to climb the rolling slopes, both Pamela and Rick slowed their mounts to a canter, and finally settled into a walk as the horses were urged onto a finely honed cow path which wound gracefully like black ribbon around the breast of the emerald hill leading into the woods beyond. Rick held back in order to fall into place beside Pamela. She looked over at him, thinking how beautifully his tan blended with the violet eyes which were shaded by the brim of his hat. Rick noticed her smile, her eyes glowing with warmth and absolute approval. He couldn't wait until she became his wife. 'I'll be the proudest man alive and the happiest. If only I wouldn't have to be caught in this dilemma regarding my brother right now! I don't want to disappear. Hopefully, when I get back she will let me explain, and will certainly understand.'

"Rick?" Pamela hesitated.

"Yes, Pamela?" Rick looked at her again, catching the scent of an orchard in delicate bloom, mingled with freshly laundered clothing. Silently he thought, 'She always smells so good!' and grinned.

"Rick, Mr. Randolph called again this morning and I've had to make a decision."

"Yes?"

She faltered, feeling miserable, wondering how she was going to keep the tears which threatened to choke her from popping to the surface. The thought of leaving him and the kids who might be orphans any day tore her heart. But, how could she stay when she needed to provide for her own child? True, only three weeks remained until the proposed wedding, but in the meantime they couldn't live on smiles, and happy days at the lakes and farms. When one walked into a store to buy milk and bread, one had to find something green with which to pay for it. Her folks had been gone for two weeks on a trip to Europe and she couldn't S.O.S. them for money. Davie wasn't a figment of her imagination. He needed, regardless of health or romance. She would just have to postpone the wedding date if need be; for the privilege of being Davie's mother was her greatest wellspring of thanksgiving to God.

"Rick, I guess I will have to return to Phoenix soon to resume my duties. Mr. Randolph's latest venture is almost completed. Also, I need to be there to successfully follow through on the work I started for him last spring."

"But I thought the doctor told you that working for another eight months, at least, is out of the question other than a few hours a day."

Wishing she could be honest and just 'poor mouth' as some folks called it, she looked down at the saddle horn watching the earth under her horse's body rise and fall, rise and fall in rhythm with the mare's hooves, withers, neck and head. She looked up at Rick through moist eyes, and saw in his magnificent square jaw a setting as if someone had slapped him hard in the face.

'I can't believe she wants to leave me,' Rick thought as he felt a stab of painful embarrassment sweeping over his senses. 'The way I've openly loved and adored you, girl? Surely you know how much I love you!' He silently writhed inside. Looking deeply into her beautiful grey eyes, trying to penetrate into her reasoning, he saw nothing... just confused tears threatening to spill over the delicate black lashes which lined the round windows of her soul. Not one to push his own way on a reluctant female who was rejecting an offer – that which was to be culminated in three weeks time – he curtly nodded his head to hide his hurt and pulled the brim of his Stetson over his eyes.

"I see!" he snapped, and with an impatient flick of reins on the mare's body, whipped past Pam down the rest of the hill onto the flat floor of the meadow. His easy grace in the saddle belied how furiously he was riding, trying to outrun the thing which was paining him as dreadfully as had his fiancée's death three years earlier.

'Is fate always going to cheat me out of my bride?' he bitterly thought as he raced headlong across the dangerously placed pocket-gopher mounds dispersed throughout the field grass. 'I thought she loved me as much as I do her. But if she does, how can she even entertain the thoughts of going back to that job before the wedding! Why can't she wait? I guess I had her figured all wrong thinking that she wanted a home and family. I don't mind her mixing a career with being a mate, nor do I mind living on my ranch on the outskirts of Scottsdale. But it's obvious that all she wants is a career. What a dad-burn fool I've been!'

Stung anew by thinking that he had been used for stud service, Rick spurred his horse into a new frenzy of speed. Memories of sweet embraces, and the passionate fire to which he had responded burned mercilessly like the tips of a million lighted cigarettes into his core. He twisted in the saddle to look back at her. She was sitting still where he had left her, looking vulnerable and bewildered, watching his receding figure.

"Go on lady! If that's what you want instead of me, get the deuce out of my life!" and anger welled in his breast threatening to choke him.

★

Pamela watched Rick race ahead of her as if stung by the very devil. His sudden look of hurt and surprise which had brought moisture into her eyes before anger overcame him, confused and hurt her. Bewilderment turned to indignation as she wiped the back of her doeskin-gloved hand across her cheek to get rid of the unwanted tears.

'So! I was just another body to you. Did you have *me* fooled, you taker, you! *No* one *ever* makes a fool out of *me*!' Stung pride bowed her head low to her heaving chest. Tossing her head back to find the reason for her agony, she saw him in the distance.

Great sadness overwhelmed her, tears poured down her face melting the grief into hot waves of fury in her chest. Pulling her mount to a halt, she softly growled:

"You will never know the full extent of my love for I shall never give it to you now. Never. You didn't even have the courtesy to allow an explanation!" Her left lung hurt. She gasped, "Furthermore, you conceited man, I will never allow you to lay as much as a finger on any part of me again. Who needs you, you arrogant lord of the manure!" Spurring her horse, she flew after Rick like a banshee.

The surge of wind created by the new burst of speed pulled the golden pin out of the top-knot of hair. Luxurious curls spilled in a shimmering shower around her shoulders only to be caught up by the flow of air into a stream of bronze behind her determined, wet face. The jewelry shook off of a sun-shot curl, flying only God knew where as its owner's hurt whipped her into submission.

Slowing to a standstill, Pamela looked mournfully at the man she loved.

She wanted to *scream* from the pain of realizing that he didn't truly love her. She was still comparatively young and tender, and had known only one man before Rick. She had never allowed herself to give her body to anyone dishonorably, and now it seemed to her as if she had. Remembering the joy with which she had given her best to Rick made fresh tears pour down her cheeks. If she hadn't loved him so completely, she never would have wanted to love him into the heavenly heights they had found in each other's arms.

'I repelled Ned's advances because his intent seemed so evil and unclean,' she dejectedly thought to herself. 'Rick with his seemingly pure motives swept me into the belief that he loved me. He even asked me to be his wife in order to deceive me into going to bed with him!' she bitterly concluded.

"I despise you!" she suddenly shouted after him.

Wheeling her horse around abruptly, heading back for the yard as fast as she could go, her mare glided over a low fence which lay around the stable yard. Pamela slowed her down, spying Sam a few yards away.

"Sam!" she jumped down from the horse, "put him away this one time, please?" She tossed the reins to the startled man.

"Sure, but the him's a her, sweetie." Then he saw her tears.

Sam quickly came over to take the reins.

"What happened, Pamela? Are you hurt?"

"Yes, but not the way you think," and she wiped an angry tear from her cheek.

"Can I help?"

"Thank you, but no, Sam. You're a dear," and she tiptoed high and gave him a quick kiss on the cheek.

With that she ran to her tiny beater. Looking over the top of the car as she opened the door, she saw Rick, half a mile away, his mare galloping toward the buildings. He was frantically waving one arm and his hat at her.

'Go find someone else!' she angrily thought to herself, jumping into her car.

Spinning out in the gravel in her haste to get away, she barreled down the driveway in a cloud of dust with never a backward glance.

'Proud Mary,' her mom had once said she should have named Pamela. For once stung, whether by something factual or imagined, it was difficult for Pamela to hang around for explanations.

★

Seeing Pamela scoot down the driveway, Rick slowed to a halt, watching her vehicle. That she was upset was obvious by the manner in which she was driving. He held his breath as she fishtailed around the corner in the loose gravel. Breathing a sigh of relief when the vehicle didn't roll over as he had anticipated, he realized that even though he was hurt into anger over her obvious rejection of him, he loved her more than he cared to admit even to himself.

Not able to see her anymore, he sadly turned to go back toward the section of fence which needed tending.

A gleam near the crest of the hill caught his eye.

Slowly walking his horse to see what it was, he looked intently at the ground. He could see only sparkles of something shining in the sun. Rising off the saddle, he got down and walked to the spot which intrigued him. Bending over to fish whatever it was out of the purple clover and yellow daisies which dotted the canary-grassed meadow, he parted the flowers with his boots.

'To think we were here just minutes ago, and so happily planning our future!' he thought to himself. 'What happened?'

Bending over, he carefully reached into an ant's jungle of dead grasses which lay unattached to the earth in a tangle of green roots and vegetating leftovers from the year before. A thistle, low and small but deadly, jammed its needles into his unsuspecting hand.

"Damn!" he exclaimed, quickly retreating to pull out the offending slivers. Whipping his leather gloves from under his belt, he smoothed them on, and bent over again to go after the tantalizing sparkles emanating from the grass. His hand touched something smooth and hard.

'Sure isn't very big,' he thought as it slipped through his gloved fingers. He took the glove off his right hand, kicked the offending thistle off its stem, and hunkered down to fish the object out. Clasping the hardness, he brought it from the tangled grasses.

A look of sorrow came into his eyes as he recognized the golden pin which Pamela always wore in her hair. It lay in the palm of his hand, the emerald which was set into a curl of gold at the head of the pin, glistened coolly in the sun.

The sight and feel of the familiar metal object catapulted his thoughts to the first time he had ever noticed it, the first time he had ever picked it up in his hand. How enchanting it had been to disentangle it from her silky tresses the first time he had ever claimed her as his own. He remembered how the cool green stone had contrasted beautifully with the copper highlights in her hair. Again he could see her as she lay in sweet ecstasy, sunshine and shadow playing over her milky body. He could almost smell the sweet hay which had been their first bed. It seemed like only yesterday, but now disbelief over what had transpired between them on the brow of this very hill only minutes ago overwhelmed him, and he wiped his gloves across his eyes. Lost in thought as he walked back toward his horse, Rick suddenly smiled.

"Yahoo!" he shouted, throwing his hat into the air. Catching it as it sailed back toward him, he grabbed his Stetson, slamming it onto his golden mane. Leaping into the saddle, he set off for home.

"Honey! You've not seen the last of me yet!" and he kissed the golden pin before tucking it into the breast pocket of his shirt next to his determined heart.

Chapter Seven

"Hi, Elsie," Pamela hastily greeted the little Swedish lady who was caring for the house in her parent's absence.

"Yah? Hello. You are home early today," she sought to make conversation with an obviously upset Pamela.

"Vould you like a cup of coffee and fresh rolls? I yust took them out of the oven."

"They smell delicious, Elsie, but thank you just the same. I'm in a hurry. Do you know where Davie is?" Pamela asked.

"Yah, that I do. I sent him out to pick the eggs. He's in the hen house I would guess from the clucking and cackling going on out there," she smiled good naturedly which lit up her little round face.

"Excuse me Elsie while I make a phone call." Pamela dialed.

"Hello. Yes, this is Pamela Ellis. I wish to make reservations to Phoenix for one adult and one child. The child is nine years old." She waited a moment. "I am hoping that you have a late flight which leaves around midnight tonight. Yes? Good!" She supplied the proper information needed, hung up the telephone and tucked a piece of paper on which she had been writing into her pocket.

Elsie looked worried.

"Pamela? Vat is dis? You are going back to Phoenix before your parents return home? Vy, they vill be so disappointed. And, you yust got here it seems."

Pamela smiled weakly.

"Elsie, I don't know how to explain right now, but if you would go round up Davie, I'd appreciate it. It's O.K. for him to finish picking the eggs. Just as long as it doesn't take too long, let him finish. Would you also supervise getting him into the tub after giving him something to eat? I'll hurry and pack, and then we have to leave in time to catch that plane. There's a four hour trip ahead of us just to get to the airport."

"Yah, yah. Sure, don't vorry about anything. I'll yust help the little shaver. I'll miss him, that's for sure. Who is going to sample my cookies and eat the mashed potatoes and gravy now?" Elsie looked sad.

Squeezing her around the shoulder with one arm, Pamela said, "Oh, you are so lovable! And, I tell you what Elsie, if you won't answer the telephone between now and the time we leave for the airport, I promise we will return for Christmas!"

"Oh, that will be yust fine! Yust fine! I'll make jule kage, krumkake, rosettes and all the things you luff the most. Yah! That vill be yust vonderful!" and Elsie started walking lightly to the kitchen, dabbing her apron at one eye.

"Are you all right?" Pamela asked sympathetically.

"Oh, Yah, yah. I yust got something in my eye," and she blew her nose sturdily, stuffing the handkerchief back into her apron pocket.

Pamela hurried upstairs. Going into the spare room, she loaded herself down with suitcases. Homesickness started settling in as she noticed the steamer trunks which she knew were stuffed with mysterious, romantic secrets which she had seen tied in pink ribbons and lace. One day she aimed to spend hours enjoying her grandmother's and grandfather's courtship.

Tossing the suitcases onto the bed in her room she snapped them open and started packing haphazardly. She raised her head abruptly as the telephone rang.

"It's him. I know it's him!" she held her breath fighting the impulse to run to the telephone. Yearning to hear his voice, yearning to make things right between them, she allowed a resurgence of hot anger to well into her chest at the remembrance of his arrogant look accompanied by the abrupt departure when she had told him of Mr. Randolph's call. She turned a deaf ear to the insistent ringing.

★

"Mom. What are you doing?" Davie stood in the doorway of his mother's bedroom, a puzzled look on his face as he stood clutching a baseball glove and assorted implements. "Where are you going, and why are you packing my clothes, too?"

Pamela looked up at her young son. "We're going back home, honey."

"But! Mom! We can't go now. I still have a month of vacation left."

"You will still have your vacation, darling. Remember all the fun you had in Phoenix last summer? Don't you miss your buddies? They'll be there to play with when we get home."

"Yes, I miss them all right, but it's hotter than blazes down there at this time of year."

"Oh, come on, sport. Don't you remember swimming all day in the pool, going to Big Surf and the golf course, not to mention going to Tucson to see Jack and Olga on the weekends. Come on, Davie. Just believe me, I must go back and get to work. We are running out of funds."

"But, I thought the doctor told you not to work for a whole year. This was sure a short year!" he grumped.

"Well, the doctor's advice would be good to follow if we could live freely. Unfortunately we can't, so I don't see that I'm not strong enough to sit on a chair behind a desk a few hours every day. I ride horse, and that's more strenuous. We just have to return, that's all there is to it."

"Oh, that's the pits!" Davie grimaced, and then shooting a challenging look at her with his green eyes, asked,

"What about Rick? How can you leave him so fast? Did you guys have a fight?"

"That, my dear boy, is none of your business, but since you asked. No. We didn't have a fight. It was just an explosion. No one said anything in anger. I wouldn't call it a fight."

"What would you call it then?"

"How about dumb?" and anger welled in her again.

"Mom. What will Grandma and Grandpa think when they come home from Europe and find us gone already? That's not very nice of us to do that."

In spite of her anger at Rick, she couldn't help but laugh at the mental jockeying her son was obviously executing.

Walking over to him to give him a hug, she said, "No matter what you say or do, we are catching that flight tonight. Now hurry, go eat, take a bath and let's shake a leg. We have to leave in less than an hour or we won't make it on time."

"Good!" he grumped as he slowly plunked down the stairs.

"Here I thought that Rick would soon be my new father," and a lump in his throat threatened to choke him. "I wish I had a dad like everyone else!" and his head hung so low he could have used his lower lip to sweep the floor.

Five hours later, Pamela and Davie pulled into the parking lot at the airport in Minneapolis.

"How are we going to get the car home, Mom?" Davie asked.

"One of your aunts is going to drive it down. She'll be starting out tomorrow, and will stay for a week or so to visit."

"I still think it's funny that we left so fast. And, even if you guys had an upset, why didn't Rick call to say goodbye to us?" Davie woefully wondered.

"He probably did, darling," Pamela sighed and averted her head, but not in time to escape notice by her son that a tear splashed onto her blouse.

By this time they had checked their baggage in the terminal. Boarding the jet seemed to take eons of time.

'I've got so much to think through that my head aches,' Pamela thought. 'The least not being Ned, who will surely come badgering me as soon as he discovers that we are home again.' The more she thought of his proposal, the more it sickened her. She sighed, leaned her head back against the seat and yielded to the delicious sensation of being rendered helpless by a friendly, powerful surge of force as the jet soared off the runway into the night. Dipping sharply to semi-circle Minneapolis, the plane straightened in its ascent into flight pattern.

Rick seemed so far away, and every second was separating them farther.

"I wonder what Rick is doing," the twenty-six year old mother sighed.

A cup of hot chocolate put spirit back into things for both travelers.

"Mom," Davie teased, "some way to raise a kid. I thought you told me that one must always take a long time to make big decisions."

"Quiet, smartie," Pamela laughed. "Do as I say, not as I do." They both laughed being it was the exact opposite of what he had always heard.

"Once in awhile, son, time waits for no one, especially your old lady. Just believe me. Everything is going to work out fine and pretty soon we will have two nickels to rub together again. Got to keep your instant oatmeal in supply, you know." She squeezed his hand, adjusted the pillow under his blond head, and said, "Sleep fast, kid."

★

Disembarking into the early morning twilight, Pamela's spirits sank even as she saw the distant mountains along which Base Line Road wound, connecting routes used to travel to Casa Grande. Even Camelback Mountain didn't charm her as it normally did when she turned around to see it kneeling majestically before the heavens in silent prayer. The castle, aglow and set like a jewel in a well-lighted case made her feel a little better.

Catching a breath of sage which the early morning softness wafted her way, she inhaled deeply, thinking of this valley in which she had lived for over ten years. The comfort which being home brought to her senses, couldn't push Rick out of her mind enough to keep the tears in check. Scanning the sunrise which lifted softly radiant arms sheathed in mother-of-pearl, she knew that at that very moment Rick was preparing to help the hired hand milk the dairy herd. A lump came into her throat as she realized that he had no idea that she was not at her folks' home. All of a sudden she regretted having left in such haste.

'He will never be able to find me. I didn't tell him where in this metropolis we live – didn't give an address, no telephone number. And, to top it off, it is an unlisted number... not that he would try to find me anyway.' She blew her nose in an already damp Kleenex. 'I must remember what a fool I was to believe he loved me. If he had loved me so much, he would have let me explain.'

She and Davie climbed into her friend Jill's engagement gift from Ned. The Porsche wound its way toward Lincoln Drive in Paradise Valley.

Chapter Eight

At that very moment twelve hundred miles distant, Rick was splashing water into his sleepy eyes. Dunking his blond curls under the water which was running from the faucet, he mumbled, "Golly, Sam. I feel like I've been run over by an elephant, and I think a whole herd ran through my mouth!" Grabbing the toothpaste and a brush, he foamed at the mouth for awhile, and came up grinning. "That feels better! Let's go milk, Sam."

"O.K. boss," Sam got up from the kitchen table where he had been indulging in a cup of strong coffee. "Want some?" he questioned, holding a mug out to Rick.

"Yes, thanks." They walked through the dewy grass, noticing the first pale peachiness of the eastern sky which framed the hills and woods beyond the east meadow. Seeing the meadow brought a quick stab of pain to Rick's heart as he remembered riding across that very place with Pamela only the morning before.

'I wonder where that girl has gone?' he thought silently. 'I couldn't get her to stop, and she shot out of here yesterday like a bat out of a hole. Thought she was going to flip out on that corner down by the highway. And, then to top it off, I kept calling her place until after midnight last night. No answer. Well, I will try again first thing after chores are done.' Thinking that Pamela reminded him of early morning sunshine, he felt a breath of hope push through the worry.

'In a few hours we'll see each other again, and this time I'm going to marry her before the day is through! No more misunderstandings. There must be a logical explanation. I didn't give her time to finish what she was going to say yesterday. I'll make up for it today, even if I have to get down on my knees and beg. I'll find out why that girl jilted me and then try to do something about it.' He smiled in anticipation knowing that he would see her in three hours.

"Come on, Sam. Let's hurry. I have a certain little lady to see this morning before I can go sit on the board of the annual meeting of the Milkers' Association."

Sam winked, and said, "Gottcha!"

Driving up the Deerfield's elm-lined driveway which curved around two acres of manicured lawn, Rick looked anxiously for Pamela's Pinto. It wasn't parked in the driveway, nor in front of the garages, nor anywhere else that he could see. The place looked deserted.

His cowboy boots sounded authoritative on the flagstones as he walked to the Georgian doors and knocked using the brass knocker. Everything was still. He heard a robin, lustily singing his little heart out, and looking toward the apple trees, saw the little fellow who was standing full-breasted and cocky with his tiny head at a tilt, listening to his next meal which was probably mindful of the robin standing on top of his turf, waiting to peck in the front door if he dared move a muscle. The robin pounced, pulling with all his might on what looked to be a fat rubber band. Rick laughed when the end of the worm snapped from the earth, popping the hardworking bird right in the head. Rick rapped a second time on the door. He heard a slow shuffle of slippers as the door started to open. A little face of Swedish extraction crinkled a sunny smile up into his face.

"Vell! If it tisn't Mr. Ricky Yarvis! Come on in, and let me fix you a cup of coffee!" Elsie insisted.

Rick followed her into the nicely appointed hall. The hardwood floors were gleaming in the morning sunshine which was spilling through the clean panes over the door.

"Is Pamela here?" Rick asked before they could reach the alcove off the kitchen where the bay window offered a cozy semi-circular table and booth snuggled opposite a fireplace.

Elsie looked fondly at Rick thinking of his parents, she replied softly, "No, Rick. She yust isn't here." Her silent thoughts continued as she envisioned Rick's brothers, sisters and aunts with whom she had shared most of her days in Minnesota. They had gone through the great depression together. Elsie chuckled remembering the discussion she and Pamela had been engaged in a couple days earlier during which Elsie was discussing Rick's family. Both families, Rick's and Pamela's grandparents, had suffered losses at that time.

"Yah," Elsie had said, "money vent so far in those days I forgot vat it looked like sometimes."

"It took a trip and just disappeared?" Pamela had laughed.

Coming back to the present, she looked at Rick across the table.

"Pamela has no idea that you are a millionaire in your own right many times over," she softly told Rick.

"I realize that," he smiled warmly at her. "I guess that is what made her so endearing. She was totally unaware of that fact, and consequently sincere in her reaction to the feelings which developed between us. That purity in a woman is hard for me to find. Most of them have been interested in the green, not the man."

Elsie contemplated the fact that she hadn't told Pamela that Rick's modest dairy operation and two thousand acres barely scratched the surface of the man's self-made empire. Pamela didn't know about the oil wells in Oklahoma in which Rick had invested while in college. Some of his investments had come up dry, but more of them had come in with black gold. He had discreetly kept that information to himself in the small Minnesota community which had been a calm oasis from a complicated, fast life in which he had found himself during and after his college days. Going to medical school hadn't helped to lend serenity to his life either; nor had his years of involvement with the State Department since coming home from serving in the Vietnam conflict.

"You know Elsie, I never was turned on to frequenting gracious drawing rooms simply because I became so sick of social mores at my mother's events as I grew up. I remember how I hated being all trussed up in formal attire, but I'd do anything for Mother. I adored her. Anyway, Pamela has obviously chosen that kind of life over what she thinks is the only thing I can give her. What's a bale of hay on which to sit in comparison to sitting on velvet, listening to the symphony?"

"Vy do you say that?" Elsie wanted to know.

"Well, you know how the men in my family are," Rick hesitated.

"How vell I know," she murmured, remembering her deceased husband-to-be.

"I love the life out of that girl, and I want her to share my millions!" he emphatically said.

"Hush now! If you brag about your vealth, it vill vanish some day."

"As I've said, you know how the men in my family are, Elsie. It's hard for us to say the things we are feeling, and sometimes we jump to conclusions, totally misunderstanding what someone is trying to tell us. And now because of that failing in myself, I've lost Pamela for sure."

"Vat makes you tink dat, Rick? Vy do you say that you've lost her?"

Rick quietly explained what had happened in the pasture the day before.

"Now that she is gone, I think I know why she took off in such a huff," he added. "You said that she flew back to Phoenix last night?"

"Yah, that she did," Elsie said softly.

"Elsie, what am I going to do now?" I've lost her." A miserable Rick squirmed in the booth.

"If someone else needs to tell you the answer to that, you don't deserve to find her, young man!" she said with a benevolent look.

"I guess you are right," Rick smiled suddenly. "You don't happen to have an address where I can find the little lady in Phoenix, do you?"

"Vy, vat makes you tink that I vould have that kind of information? And, vat makes you tink that I vould ever give it to the likes of you?" she laughed before sipping more coffee from her china saucer through the sugar lump held between her front teeth.

"Anyone else would look sloppy sipping their coffee like that, Elsie," Rick teased. "But, you have always had such grace. How do you do that without losing half the coffee out of your mouth?"

"O.K., O.K. That is enough flattery. It will get you everything you vant from me. I'll get you the address. But, if I give it to you and don't see that pretty little voman and her boy back here inside of a mont, I will personally take you to task." She laughed merrily, bustling over to the kitchen desk made of maplewood. Pulling out a drawer she took a yellow book into her hand. "Here it tis," and she brought the address book, a piece of paper and a pen to Rick who hastily jotted the information.

"I have to dash. Have a meeting to attend, and then I am going to go home, pack a duffel bag and fly down there to get that gal, if she will have me," Rick announced. "Thanks, my almost great aunt Elsie!" and he picked her up off the floor, and planted a kiss squarely on her little dimpled cheek, "Thanks for the Swedish tea ring," he said as he picked up a piece of the soft, frosted bread which she had just finished making before his arrival. "I feel better already."

"Go on, you scalawag!" she laughed, and scooted him out the door with a pat on his jeaned bottom.

"Call Sam, and tell him to get the Lear ready, will you Elsie? I want to leave for the Southwest as soon as the dairy meeting is over at noon."

"Yah! Yah! Vork me to death, vill you. Sure. I'll do it. Good luck, Rick," she happily waved him off as he took to the road in his favorite camouflage, the old beater.

★

Hurrying home after the meeting, Rick found Sam and told him to load the bags he hurriedly packed in order to have enough time to make arrangements with his sister who said she would care for the children until he came back.

"You don't mind being available for any incoming calls regarding Don and Sis, do you?" he asked.

"Of course not," his eldest sister replied.

"Here's my number at the ranch down there, course you already have it," he smiled.

Sitting down on the edge of the bed, he dialed the Phoenix area number which Elsie had given him that morning.

"Hello," a lovely voice said from the other end.

"Hello, Ma'am. My name is Rick."

"Oh, Rick! Yes, Pamela has told me about you," the lady said happily.

"She has? And to whom am I speaking, please? Your name was not included with the number which a mutual friend of Pam's and mine gave to me in order that I might find her."

"My name is Jill Farthing."

"Jill Farthing? Why Pamela has told me that you are her dearest friend. Oh, yes, I have heard many good things about you."

"Why, thank you." Jill was obviously pleased. "And, may I say that I am absolutely thrilled that you have called this afternoon? I have been wishing ever since Pamela's return that I could talk with you."

A faint hope that perhaps Pamela had expressed a need for him passed through Rick's mind. "And, how could I be of assistance, Jill?"

"Well, I was wondering if you would be able to come down here for a few days. I am getting married the end of this week on Saturday morning, and would be so pleased if you would attend the wedding. Pamela is coming, acting as my matron of honor, although she resisted the idea in favor of going to Chicago on a buying trip for her employer. I didn't take offense at her suggestion, although it saddened me. I understand why a wedding would be difficult for her at the present time, thinking that it had to do with her husband's passing a couple of years ago. However," she hesitated,

"However what?" Rick asked.

"However, I have become aware since, that it is not the memories of that long ago which are disturbing her. The memories which are causing such distress are still warm from being so newly made," she added softly.

Rick understood her meaning. Could it be that Pamela was missing him as much as he was missing her?

"I guess both of us are unhappy for the same reason," Rick said. "That is why I am leaving in a few minutes to come down to find her. But, please don't tell her that I am on the way. I need to deal with this on my own terms."

"Well then," Jill pursued, "when you touch down, why don't you call me again, and we can go from there as to how and where to find Pamela?" She proceeded to give him her shop address and number.

"Sounds as if you're right next to Goldwater's department store near Central and Camelback!"

"That I am, sir!" she jauntily replied.

"What do you sell, if I may ask? Anything fitting for a pretty grey-eyed lady whose eyes could melt a heart of steel?"

Jill laughed quietly. "Oh, yes. Everything from fine jewelry to exquisite personal apparel is here for the offing."

"Well then, from the airport I'll come straight to your shop to buy my lady-love something pretty!"

"That will be wonderful, Rick. I'll look forward to meeting you tonight. In fact, I'll stay over just for you. But, do hurry as I have to deliver a few bridesmaid gowns before going home this evening."

"No problem, Jill. I'll be there quick as a flash and we'll get acquainted over a few pieces of finery, and plot our surprise for Pamela."

With that they hung up, both smiling – one exultantly, the other quietly with a dreamy look of satisfaction in her eyes.

'Oh, Pamela!' she thought to herself. 'Are you in for a treat. I am so happy for you!'

No sooner had the thought passed through her mind than the telephone rang again. Picking it up she heard Ned's silky voice saying:

"Darling? I hope you won't mind, but I can't make our dinner engagement tonight. I have been called to Mexico City suddenly and must leave in half an hour."

"But sweetheart," Jill faltered, "we were supposed to meet with the priest to choose our ceremonial vows and service. We only have a couple of days left in which to do so."

"I know, darling. But you know how important it is to attend updates in relation to our cartel imports."

"Yes, I know. When will you be returning?"

"Evening after next. I'll be able to get home for the little rehearsal you have planned. Then, my dear, may I have the pleasure of your company all to myself for the remainder of the night?"

"That depends upon how short you propose that night should be," she teased. "I must get my beauty sleep you know. I don't want to be the first bride in the Phoenix area to have bags under her eyes for the bridal mass."

"I promise to leave at the stroke of midnight, before your coach turns into a pumpkin and your footmen become lizards, and all the horses turn into mice," Ned whispered in her ear. "Just as long as I get to keep the glass slipper until I can slip it on your foot Saturday morning, that is all I care about at this point," he seductively concluded.

"Yes, Ned. The slipper is yours, and I shall wait to see you day after tomorrow. But, it is hard to be patient! Two days seem like an eternity at this point."

"It seems as such to me as well, my lovely dove. But I shall be thinking of you and only you every moment from the time we finish this conversation until I can take you into my arms again. You are on my mind constantly. There is no other, my darling."

"Oh, Ned. I do love you. Please hurry back."

"Yes, darling. Goodbye." And the receiver went dead in Jill's hand. Quietly replacing it into the cradle, she sighed with disappointment and then looked over at the bridal section of the shop where she could see the ethereal folds of white silk which made up the skirt of her wedding gown peeping from behind the oriental ricepaper screen. The birds and mimosa branches painted on the screen were etched in gold leaf and she wondered if any shy, young Japanese bride had ever donned her red wedding silks behind the delicate panels even as she who would be slipping into her gown behind its sheltering arms. She smiled mystically, for she was a romantic. Her eyes traveled to the sea-green chiffon creation in which Pamela would be draped. Walking to it, she let her hand linger lovingly on the Grecian crossover on the bodice and to the golden clasp on the shoulder where a spray of chiffon was caught before flowing over the shoulder into six feet of classical folds.

'Goodness, but you will look lovely in this, Pamela,' she thought silently. 'Rick is in for a breathtaking treat, what with your auburn hair and grey eyes. This color will even bring subtle shades of green into those chameleon eyes of yours.' She smiled, and was happy for her dearest friend. 'We must sweep those burnished curls up and entwine green jewels through them, topping the creation with the golden pin to which you are partial.' And Jill proceeded to pull plastic garment bags over the gowns.

'I've not told Pamela that I am bringing this over tonight. Perhaps I ought to call now while the shop is empty.'

She started walking to the telephone, but the tinkle of the brass bell on the door caught her attention as two matrons dressed to the nines walked in. Nodding politely at Jill, they walked regally in their fashionable clothes to the racks which held the latest creations from Paris.

Jill caught her breath when she first sighted the gigantic diamond solitaire on the short one's beautifully manicured, dimpled little hand. Her red fingernails looked wet and deliciously rich as they moved over the hangers, grasping first one and then another dress which caught her fancy.

"Dahling," the black headed shopper drawled in Brooklynese, "isn't this absolutely lovely?"

"Oh, yes it is," Jill responded with an unaffected smile. "Would you like to try it on?"

"Yes, dahling. And I will take a few more with me at the same time." Her eyes twinkled merrily, and she added, "I just hate to wriggle in and out of the dress I'm presently wearing, so if I take a whole armful from the rack at one time, I can leave it off until I try on everything. That way it doesn't become such an exhausting job to continue being fetching for my husband!" and she laughed heartily. "What we don't go through to be beautiful!" and she tap-tapped sharply to the dressing room on spike-heeled shoes, her well endowed and girdled derriere bobbing.

On the way to try on the clothes from the rack the lady spied a leather jacket under which were brushed denim jeans and a matching brown cowboy shirt. Tiger-eye snaps gave a simple touch of class to the outfit, not that the beaded doe skin jacket's creamy color and texture didn't take one's breath away.

"My goodness, how I wish I could ride a hoss!" she exclaimed. "I'd buy that outfit, boots and all in a wink!" her little red mouth made a perfect 'O'. "Of course, I don't think I could fit this into those jeans, nor a saddle either, for that matter," she lamented as she patted her backside. Jill could hardly keep from laughing but managed to bury a giggle in a sneeze, thanks to a hastily grabbed tissue from her pocket.

By the time the various customers who had filtered in during the afternoon had satisfied their desires, Jill was happy that it was five o'clock and that she could turn the main lights in the building low to wait for Rick. Wondering what he would look like, she carried her purse and wedding paraphernalia to the rear of the shop, hanging them by the door where she could grab them easily on her way to Pamela's. The telephone rang.

"Jill?" a breathless Pamela inquired.

"Yes, Pamela?"

"I know that this is short notice, but could you come over in about an hour?"

"Why yes, as a matter of fact, I could. I was planning to pop by with your dress anyway," she hesitated. "I may be late though."

"Oh, that's O.K.!" Pamela exclaimed. "Don't eat anything on the way, all right? Maybe we can go eat after a few drinks. Would you like that?"

"Yes. I would be delighted."

"O.K. I will see you soon," and an obviously excited Pamela hung up the telephone.

"I wonder why she is so excited," Jill mused. "That girl always has something up her sleeve over which to be enthused."

★

After introducing himself to Jill via the telephone, Rick hurriedly dug in his closet and found a blue-grey suit cut superbly in the western tradition, took a shirt of white silk with pearlized stripes out of a drawer, found the proper tie, and dove-grey boots. Shining their snake skin tops with his sleeve while admiring the shades of white, black and grey which Mother Nature had endowed upon the slithery scourge of mankind, he encased all in a leather bag. Carefully securing the golden pin into the pen hole in the shirt pocket, he zipped the side compartment.

"Now, where do I put my grey hat?" he wondered. "Well, if I wear these grey pants and kid jacket over this baby-blue shirt, it'll go fine and I can wear it on my head instead of the sage hat." So thinking, he hurried into the shower.

Finally dressed with bags in hand, the telephone demanded his attention.

"Hello," he answered impatiently. "You what? You think you have found a way to get my brother and his wife home?" He listened for awhile. "Well, if it is going to take twelve hours before you can tell me anything definite, I will give you a different number at which I may be reached later tonight. This can be taken care of as well from Phoenix if not better than from this little isolated hamlet up north, don't you agree? O.K. That's fine. I'll be anxiously waiting for your call."

He gave the caller his Phoenix telephone number and hung up with a sigh of relief.

"Well, it looks as if I might have to put my itty-bitty on the line again, and endure a taste of hell in getting them safely home, but it will be worth it." Hurrying downstairs to find his sister, he explained the call and the request which the caller had made.

"He asked if I'd be willing to fly over to West Africa in order to pick them up after they've been smuggled into an escape route near the coast. We will have to go under cover of darkness." He looked anxiously at his sister. "Can you manage the kids while I am gone?" he gently asked.

"Sure," she smiled through worried tears. "But I wish all three of you, *two* brothers and a sister-in-law, didn't have to be actively involved."

"Oh, darlin'," he grinned, tweaking her nose, "have you ever seen a time that I didn't make it out of a scrape?"

"No, that I haven't," she softly replied. Suddenly she threw her arms around his neck. "Do you *have* to go?"

"As it looks now, I'm afraid so. But, maybe things will change by tonight when they call me in Phoenix."

"Well, I for one am going to be praying towards that end. Surely they don't need to endanger your life also in order to save the other two. We need you here if the attempt fails, Rick."

He held her away from him, looking with brotherly love into the face of his lovely and wise older sister.

"I'll be careful and I will come home to all of you, I promise." Then he suddenly grinned. "And, if I am lucky and the gods are with me, I'll be bringing the sweetest gal this side of heaven back with me plus that little calf of hers, of course! Not to mention the fact that Don and Sis will come home to the kids."

Giving one last goodbye hug, he told her to tell the brood goodbye for him. By now, all four children had gotten used to their gregarious uncle's sudden comings and goings, and it made them just love him all the more to think that he was so important.

"Makes a feller wonder how to pack. How'd I get into going to a wedding and a possible rescue operation when all I wanted to do was go find that girl of mine and persuade her to come home?" He jumped into his modest beater and drove out to the highway.

After driving thirty miles more or less, Minnesota's rolling hills rolled one last time into flatlands of rich, black loam – the fabled Red River of the North's donation of enriched silt left by centuries of lazing and rampaging along.

Frequent flooding was caused by annual melting snowdrifts sometimes piled as high as a Dakota or Minnesota rooftop. Ancient Glacial Lake Agassiz, the two million square kilometer leftover from the Ice Age Meltdown had found her resting place here. The fresh water lake bed had extended over parts of what Rick knew as the states of Minnesota, North and South Dakota. As time passed, the huge lake both dried and ran into tributaries which emptied into the northward flow of the Red River to what became known as Canada. Eventually Lake Agassiz (daughter of the Des Moines Lobe of the Wisconsin glaciation born eleven thousand, seven hundred years ago) was no more. But her legacy, the flat banks of the river extending farther than the eye could see, was *still* making wealth for the sons of the nineteenth century pioneers who had plowed and reaped from sprawling Agassiz' birthing bed of black gold.

'This Red River Valley may be flatter than my sis's pancakes, but I sure do love it. I can see forever when heading west.' The sun was bright, and puffy cumulus humilis filled the blue skies, which relaxed Rick a little. As it was, he would barely make Phoenix in time to go to Jill's shop by the hour specified.

Arriving at the airport in Fargo, North Dakota, Rick lumbered into the parking lot at the helm of the old red truck, ground it to a stop and jumped out. With bag in hand, he hurried to the jet and climbing in beside Sam, said "Can't leave without my first mate, right?"

Sam smiled, in response to the captain of the Lear.

"No, and what is more, I don't mind being co-pilot whenever you take a mind to navigate. In fact, I wish you'd do it more often. Reminds me of our days in Nam."

"Yes, those were sad days, weren't they. But, that's where I found you, and you are about the best buddy a fellow could ever hope for."

Soon they were high over the Dakotas, discussing the telephone call regarding Rick's brother and sister-in-law.

"If you go, I go," Sam firmly said.

"Awe, shucks! You don't have to do that."

"Yes, I do. We've always stuck together, Rick. You saved my life once, remember? Now it's my turn, and I *am*

not going to stay at home. Don't say another word, friend!"
They looked at each other, and clasped hands, cementing
the feelings which were strong between them.

★

Jill looked up as a shadow caught her eye. There stood a
tall, handsome man with a square jaw, tanned face and the
most gorgeous violet eyes she had ever seen. In fact, she
had never seen any before, just had heard of such mythical
wonders in the human race.

'Wow! What a beautiful man!' she thought to herself as
she smiled, and crossed over the parquet floor to unlock the
door.

"With a grin like that, and eyes like those, I think you are
the embodiment of Pamela's explanations," she said gaily.
"Come in."

"Don't mind if I do, and thank you. Jill, is it?"

"Yes", she softly smiled. They shook hands.

After talking for awhile, Rick strolled languidly over
towards the lingerie section.

"What I would like to find, if you have them, would be a
midnight lavender gown and peignoir, and a few pieces of
amethyst jewelry set in gold. Would you happen to have
anything to fit that description?"

"Oh, I think I might," Jill smiled. "It wouldn't have
anything to do with those unusually beautiful eyes of yours,
would it?" She smiled into their violet depths.

"Well, just maybe. Just maybe," he laughed self-
consciously. "With neither you nor I telling her that I am
here for a couple of days, I thought maybe I could leave a
clue now and then. I thought I would start with this," and
he pulled the gold and emerald pin from his shirt pocket.

"Oh! You found it!" Jill breathlessly explained. "Oh, Pamela will be so overjoyed, Rick! She thought it was gone forever because she said that it must have fallen out of her hair when she was dashing across the meadow at your place." Suddenly blushing for fear she had given away a confidence which would have been better left unrecalled, she ducked her blond head.

"Hey, don't be embarrassed. It's O.K. Yes, I just happened to see something glittering in the sun, down in the grass and weeds. I got off my horse, felt around a little bit and came up with this lovely thing. And, if you'd be my co-conspirator, I intend to lay it on her pillow before she goes to bed tonight – without her seeing me, of course," he smiled invitingly. "Want to join me in surprising her?"

"Oh, yes! How romantic! I still have a house key which she insisted I keep and use at my own discretion even though I've moved my things to Ned's place. Well, this is certainly one of the best reasons I can think of for using the key."

Carefully selecting a creation of violet silk charmeuse overlaid with a whisper of silver-grey chiffon, Rick held out the yards of material which were gathered enchantingly from the simple, low neckline across the back. He decided that the subdued violet-grey ensemble would look wondrously fair when worn by his grey eyed love. He could visualize her in its loveliness and see the delicate slivery touches of thin lace on her wrists and bosom. Thoughts of her silky mass of curls lying loosely across her shoulders in this lovely rhapsody of nighttime colors made his head quicken.

"Excuse me, Rick?" Jill interrupted his thoughts.

Ducking his head a little to push the brim of his hat back a bit in embarrassment, he cleared his throat and set about asking for matching silver sandals, and the jewelry. Going over to the jewelry cases, he carefully examined the amethysts.

"I especially like these," he decided, picking up a thick, but delicate yellow gold and platinum chain which had a pear cut amethyst where both sides of the chain met, creating a graceful V. The necklace was made to keep its shape, and to drop slightly above a low décolletage. He picked up the matching earrings which were delicately wrought.

"Would you be interested in this also?" Jill asked, reaching into the case to bring out a hair pin which was simply but beautifully made to match the others.

"Why, look at that! Yes, I would like to add that to this little collection," he said, thinking how he would enjoy seeing something which *he* had given her gracing her pretty head.

Looking around a bit, Rick continued, "By the way, where could I find a little something for that tadpole of hers?"

Finally the gifts were wrapped. All the shopping was done. Giving Rick directions and leaving Pamela's key in his safekeeping, they walked out to her car.

"Where is your car, Rick?"

"Oh, here it comes now," Rick replied. "My partner took it to run an errand while I was with you. As a matter of fact, I want you to meet him. He's the best friend I have and my business partner."

A teal blue luxury car pulled up beside them.

"Howdy, pardner!" the black-headed man with blue eyes smiled through the descending window. "Am I late?"

"No, no. As a matter of fact your timing couldn't have been more perfect," Rick grinned. "Jill, I would like you to say hello to Sam McClintock, my business partner and friend. Sam, Jill," and he finished the introduction.

In spite of her plans to wed in a matter of days, Jill felt herself drawn to the man whom she was meeting. She felt shaken and for the first time, the hesitation over marrying Ned which she had been feeling ever since he had suddenly disappeared a few weeks earlier during her buying trip to New York, became a clear statement in her mind. Quietly, she thought to herself that she must think things through to her satisfaction before finalizing her commitment to Ned that coming weekend. But, she loved Ned and love makes excuses.

"Pleased to meet you. I trust I will see you at the wedding in a couple of days," she smiled, excusing herself as she went to her car. Carefully lying her wedding dress and Pamela's gown in the passenger seat, she waved goodbye to the fellows and left.

'Yes! I really must face my feelings!' she thought to herself as she drove along Camelback toward 40th Street. 'Something about Ned's behavior has really been bothering me and I have not wanted to admit it before.' She geared down to stop at a red light. 'I just don't understand his sudden need to attend conventions, or meet business partners in the middle of the evenings. And, why must he jaunt off to Mexico City barely two days before the wedding? I might love him, but I don't trust the man. So, why am I marrying him?' She contemplated awhile as she drove along. 'I'm marrying him because I love him and because his good points outweigh his questionable acts.'

She turned toward Paradise Valley, enjoying the dips in the road through which spring rains-turned-torrents swept in frenzied rivers during sudden storms carrying everything in its wake which happened to be in the wash.

'Sometimes I think he fools around with some other woman. The things he says just don't stack up.'

Pulling into Pamela's drive, she stopped in front of the stucco, Spanish style town house. 'I sure love the red tile roof,' Jill thought as she opened the door to get out. All of a sudden she felt her recent fears regarding Ned being fed as she recognized his car parked across the parking lot.

'That is Ned's car! He is supposed to be on his way to Mexico! What is he doing here?' With a thumping heart she gathered the foamy, cool-looking green dress in her arms from the passenger seat and slowly locked her door. Taking a deep breath to quell the sick feeling which had attacked the pit of her stomach, she walked over to Ned's car.

'It's his all right,' she thought. 'I wonder who he is visiting in this particular complex. The only person we know here is Pamela.'

At that thought, a stab of jealousy charged through her heart. 'Not Pamela! Oh, certainly not Pamela! And even if he is visiting her, it would not be for any devious reason on Pamela's part, I am sure of that. But, on his? Well, that is another matter. I am not quite as naïve as he makes me out to be, and I have noticed all too often how he disappears from a room if Pamela has walked out to get something. Come to think of it, she invariably gets into a bad temper when he is around. I wonder...' and with that she rang the doorbell... 'I wonder if she has been trying to tell me something without actually making an accusation so as not to hurt my feelings.'

Deciding that Pamela loved Rick and that Ned was barking up the wrong tree even if he was trying to clandestinely woo Pamela, Jill thought, 'Well, some men must play until caught with their hand in the cookie jar, I suppose. So, if he is sorry, and will mend his ways, the wedding will go on!'

The heavy door swung open, revealing a relieved-looking Pamela.

'Oh, Jill!' she thought as she looked at her dearest friend. 'If only I could take a minute to tell you that Ned called me to get an answer to an indecent proposal which he offered not long ago.' Worriedly looking at her friend, she reflected on the afternoon's events, hiding her concern with a cheerful hello. She could still hear the exchange between herself and Ned when she had said in response to his persistent call:

"Ned, I promised you that I would think over your proposition and give you a final answer. But, you lied. You are not married."

"Yes, my dear," his voice had smoothly flowed over the wires into what seemed the very core of her, making her feel chilly with dislike. "Jill mentioned that you saw the doctor recently. Does your decision have anything to do with what he told you?"

Wondering what in the world that would have to do with anything, Pamela answered, "Of course not."

"I see," he softly breathed. "Of course if you were restricted from working because of additional injuries received while bouncing around on a horse when you were supposed to be recuperating, it wouldn't cause you to choose security."

His gentle sarcasm hit home. Already she felt sick in the pit of her stomach from the anxiety regarding finances which seemed to be plaguing her ever since she returned from the clinic where, to her surprise, she had been examined by someone other than her surgeon.

"I'll make it. I always have and I always will," she sharply responded.

"You'll make it all right. Just like a butterfly with a broken wing. Without my help you will *not* make it. Is that what you want for David?"

"I am not a butterfly with a broken wing and even if I were, broken wings have been known to heal!" she snapped.

"Just the same as a broken heart?" he softly persisted, knowing that he was touching a vulnerable area.

"And, what do you mean by that remark?" she indignantly asked.

"Oh, nothing of much consequence. But there doesn't seem to be any boot marks outside your door in the desert sand, nor cowboy gear hanging inside on the hall stand. No phone calls from the male gender either, at least not from the 218 area code."

"Why, you dishonorable gentleman!" she exclaimed, in exasperation.

Ned chuckled at the obvious contradiction in her choice of words.

In a fury Pamela continued, "You assured me that you would not spy on me anymore. How do you know what I am doing or not doing?"

"It is my business to know. I take care of my interests."

"It is *not* your business to know and I am *not* any concern of yours." She continued, "I am so relieved that I did not consider your offer at all for it seemed preposterous to me. I just told you that I would consider it to get you out of my hair! I would *never* do such a thing to Jill. As a matter of fact, I intend to tell her unless, of course, you mend your ways. As I said, the only way to effect your departure from my parent's home without making a scene the night you asked, was to promise I would give it some thought."

"Ah, my dear. That was a mistake," he quietly said.

She could tell that he was angered because he always spoke practically in a whisper when fury was surging through his volcanic nature.

"I am coming over immediately!" he said and before she could answer, there was a click and the phone went silent in her hand.

'Oh, Lordy. Now what shall I do, where can I go?' she frantically looked around the room. 'Oh, this is silly of me, perfectly silly. Let him come. What difference will it make? I will just call Jill and invite her over also! Of course, I'll not tell him that I have done so. What a delicious jolt for Ned when she appears at the door!' She smiled to herself. 'He will be a perfect gentleman in front of her and perhaps she will take the hint and start questioning why he is here at all.'

Feeling like an impish little she-devil all of a sudden, she decided to freshen her make-up and put on a high-necked, long-sleeved, soft grey blouse which was especially provocative in order to tease the lion a little.

'He thinks he orders the sun, moon and stars! Well. This is one lady he doesn't control!' She put a touch of amber liquid behind her ears which filled the room with the scent of a richly aged, floral sherry.

'My favorite. At one hundred and twenty-seven dollars an ounce, I must use you sparingly until better times return. Davie's daddy gave me this,' she remembered as tears misted her eyes. She lightly kissed the crystal container, smoothing the gold plaque bearing its name with one frosted finger tip. Smiling at herself one last time in the mirror, she went to answer the doorbell.

'Eat your heart out,' she thought, as she faced the darkly scowling Spaniard at the door.

The silk draped over her full loveliness caused the desired effect. He visibly softened, looking with admiration and respect at the strong little woman who dared defy not only him to protect a friend, but also the odds which had been and still were stacked against her son and herself.

To think that she might not survive the injuries which had been sustained in the car accident if she did not take proper care of herself, was a thought which truly pained him. Looking at the lovely vision which she made in the doorway, he felt an overwhelming desire to take care of her. The grey in her blouse brought out the spiritual quality in her eyes which he loved so well. If only he hadn't rushed into a proposal of marriage to Jill, for he now felt that given a little time, Pamela would have changed her mind about him. But it was too late now.

'Now I must persuade her to let me care for her needs. Dr. Koss emphasized that she must not exert herself for some time as she did this past summer. I must talk her into becoming my charge in some fashion. And, somehow! Jill or no Jill, I must possess this little spitfire standing in front of me!'

With a sparkle in her eyes, she gaily showed him in. Softly shutting the heavily carved door, she followed him across the Mexican tiles which felt cool under the thin soles of her high-heeled sandals which matched the white silk and soft grey trim of her straight skirt. A wide silver belt made of coins encircled her tiny waist and as she passed to walk in front of him to the living room, he feasted his eyes on the lovely roundness of her hips and the long legs which had always interested him.

'She certainly is lovely today,' he thought, catching a faint breath of her perfume. Recognizing it as the most expensive scent one could buy, he smiled wryly to himself. 'Now, how is a woman with such obvious expensive taste going to survive without her apprentice decorator's income for a whole year?' Miscalculating her character which also had a wide streak of pioneer blood mixed into it from her great-grandfathers and mother, he congratulated himself that he was about to enjoy a piece of cake. 'No contest,' he thought to himself.

"Please have a seat, Ned," Pamela purred. "Would you like a glass of wine? I have your favorite here. There is still half a bottle left over from the dinner which Jill and I made for you before I went to Minnesota." Suddenly thinking that it might be somewhat flat by now, she started to laugh as she poured it into a wine glass. She hadn't meant to be rude by offering inferior wine, but it seemed to fit the occasion as an understatement of her feelings at the moment.

"Thank you," he took the crystal goblet from her hand. The sun, shining in a golden shaft diagonally through the room caught the wine's full color causing reflections of ruby red to bounce from prism to prism beneath the smooth, thin rim. The liquid stirred slightly, as did the depths of his eyes as he looked at Pamela who was looking into his face, laugh dimples at the corners of her mouth threatening to deepen. Her grey eyes were twinkling with suppressed mirth and she dared not say a word lest she lose the battle. Seeing the restrained gaiety, Ned was relieved for he had not wanted to offend the girl. He truly cared for her.

Ned's intentions had been good, but thwarted by her loyalty to Jill, his ancestral drive to capture, hold and enjoy while taming had come into the fore. His family had always taken what they wanted, if what they desired would not come willingly, or did not belong to them. Honorable battle was done for lands and vineyards centuries ago. Marriages were made to accommodate desires if no alliances to protect borders were necessary. If that latter was not the case, a mistress, a lovematch if you will, was expected... a lifelong love match. 'One life, one love,' his father had always said.

To Pamela, one life, one love meant something entirely different. She didn't understand his ancient culture to the point where she could participate without feeling great shame, guilt and a sense of worthlessness. Ned, on the other hand, understood her sense of values, although in trying to persuade her into his lair, he pretended that he did not. Pamela felt that if she wasn't good enough to be a man's wife, then she didn't want to take a place as a love mate only. They were of two different cultures, two different minds.

Pamela watched Ned take a sip of the wine. He watched her watching him, aware that surely by now the wine would be flatter than her beloved cowboy's flapjacks. Pretending that he did not notice, he set the glass on the mahogany console piano. Their eyes met, and Pamela's nature got the best of her. She started to laugh along with Ned who couldn't help but enjoy her unpretentious ways. He knew that she was unsophisticated enough to have forgotten that a bottle of wine which had been opened and sitting in the refrigerator for a few odd months might just not be the taste of the year.

"Oh, Ned. I am sorry, truly I am. I didn't even think until I had already offered it to you. I just remembered that I had the brand your preferred in the fridge."

"It's all right. What else do you have in this lovely apartment of yours? Knowing you, I bet there is a bottle of Red DuBonnet lurking about somewhere. Or, are you saving it for Christmas, as is your wont?"

He walked over to the liquor cabinet and opening the door, said, "Aha! We are in luck. There are two perfectly good wines here. Which do you prefer, the Rhine wine or the DuBonnet... or are you saving the DuBonnet to savor over *War and Peace*, again?"

"Which one would you like the most, Ned?" Pamela asked, truly preferring that he have his choice.

"Well, I do like the DuBonnet at this time of day. It is a light, late afternoon drink which doesn't require canapés to make it seem at its best."

Pamela went to fetch ice for herself. Filling a silver bucket and dropping a few pieces into the crystal goblets, she carried it all back to the white carpeted living room on a silver tray, hoping that Jill would hurry.

Noticing that she had placed three glasses on the tray instead of two, Ned asked, "Are you expecting someone else?"

"As a matter of fact, yes I am, and she is here now."

Going to answer the door in response to the bell, she victoriously smiled at a disappointed Ned.

Chapter Nine

"Do come in, Jill dear," Pamela said.

Ned's black eyebrows drew together momentarily, but immediately the scowl was replaced by a look of radiant, joyous surprise, his demeanor impeccable.

The ladies came into the room where Ned looked up smiling.

"Hi, darling," he said comfortably. Busily pouring the wine, he pretended not to see his fiancée's shocked expression.

Jill exclaimed, "Oh! What a splendid surprise, Pamela!" And then to her husband-to-be, "You are so full of fun, darling. I expected you to be in Mexico City by now as you previously mentioned. How happy I am that you are here instead. I just hate it when you have to jet off at the drop of a hat!" and she perfunctorily kissed him.

Tousling his coiffed hair which absolutely drove him up the wall causing little jerks to ripple under the skin of his left cheek, she innocently asked, "What happened? Why are you allowed to stay home this time? How good of them to share you with me, especially two days before our nuptuals... or is it one and a half?"

With tremendous effort he smiled, smoothing his hair.

"It's good to see you, dear. Will you have a glass of wine?" and so saying, placed a sherry glass in her hand.

Ned looked over his fiancée's head at Pamela who was standing triumphantly a few paces behind Jill. If looks could have spoken, the word 'touché' would have resounded from wall to wall in the quiet room. Ned tilted his head and glass silently in salute to Pamela's coup-de-grace.

'Clever lady,' he admiringly and ruefully thought.

"Why don't we all sit down and enjoy ourselves?" the hostess suggested.

Jill chose a white silk chair which was placed in conjunction with Pamela's favorite oil painting. A modern piece which her sister had painted on a blazing red background depicting the charred ruins of a huge tree. The sun's rays filtered through the hell, promising new life to the blackened remains and devastated landscape. Looking at it always renewed Pamela's sense of survival and in that scene the scripture in Isaiah which promised to give those who mourn, 'beauty for ashes', came alive. The picture was toned into acceptance by the deep brown of the wall on which it was hanging and cooled by the icy white chair and carpeting. Warm, rich mahogany and lamps tastefully chosen for strategic yet subtle effect filled the room with gentle soft grace.

There were books on inconspicuous shelves, minute crystal ashtrays which were solid enough to give pleasure to men, yet pretty enough to intrigue a woman. Rich browns and shades of red occasionally added dashes, as if thrown there by a flamboyant chef adding spices to his favorite dish in a gourmet kitchen, making the room comfortably rich.

Ned sat on the deep brown couch, a cherry red pillow brushing his tan arm on which warmly glowed a yellow gold chain inside of which was concealed a small watch. Pamela had been fascinated by the clever piece of jewelry upon meeting him months ago. Slowly sinking onto a burgundy ottoman, she leaned against the matching chair's arm crossing her shapely ankles.

"Would anyone like crackers and cheese?" she asked. "I'll not use the word canapés, for when I'm with you it is easy to make it old home week by using the everyday language of my Minnesota farm home."

"Although that is a pleasant suggestion, I don't care for any, thank you," Ned replied.

"Nor I," Jill enjoined.

"Knowing you, the cheese and the crackers have probably been in the refrigerator for three months and by now sport a layer of green," Ned teased darkly.

Laughing at his smart remark, Pamela countered, "Good. Maybe we can make some penicillin with which to clear an infected relationship."

Jill colored slightly, took Ned's hand humbly and said, "Darling, we can discuss this later."

"Of course," he charmingly acquiesced deciding that he shouldn't have been so dumb as to have been caught trying to woo Jill's dearest friend. 'But Jill is so innocent, she doesn't know.'

Walking across the room Ned stood, hands in his tan slack pockets examining a painting of Jill.

"Now, let's get down to the truly interesting events which are about to occur," Pamela suggested.

In spite of her earlier misgivings, Jill smiled radiantly across the room at Ned. All her anxieties fled for a time at least. Right now, she had something to accomplish and that was to make sure that Pamela accepted the request of being matron of honor at the nuptials. She had to make sure that Ned accepted the idea of Rick standing as best man... yes, she had much to persuade.

"You're speaking of the wedding, aren't you Pamela," she said.

"Yes, I am. You are going to be a perfect bride, you are blushing already!" They laughed. "Why the blush, Jill? Do tell what marvelous little secret brings that glow to your cheeks and eyes!" Pamela teased.

Ned fidgeted with the goblet between his hands, watching the red liquid as it licked the sides into wet, mercurial semicircles which almost touched the rim before sliding back down the sides of the glass.

'There is a potential tempest in each calm pool, it would seem,' he silently thought to himself as he raised his eyes to study Pamela. 'To what is she referring?' He settled back with his drink, crossing his legs. His spit-polished shoe reflected a prism of light which bounced off a crystal paperweight on which was etched the virginal portrayal of Virgo calmly petting the mane of a Scorpio lion. They were resting beside each other on the banks of a stream. He looked at it and was struck by its accuracy in depicting the object of his admiration in whose home he was now relaxing.

'She tames the beast in most people, come to think of it.' He looked at her again. There was that patient, somewhat spiritual essence in the depths of her eyes which attracted him immensely. Jill did not have that quality, although she was an absolutely lovely and sensitive person inside and out. Pamela could also be an imp, though, which he relished without question.

'Ah, well, what does it matter? She has made her wishes abundantly clear. I must respect the strength of character in her and abide by those unspoken wishes. However, perhaps I can persuade her to let me at least help with her son. I love that child. He reminds me of myself when I was his age. Perhaps Pamela would consent in allowing Jill and me to raise him until she has recuperated enough to become established. I must ask her, but I want to do so when we are alone.' Knowing that Jill would automatically agree to the idea because of her love for Pamela and Davie, he concentrated on the girls' feverish excitement over the impending ceremonies.

"You will attend the wedding, won't you Pamela?" Jill breathlessly asked.

Laughing, Pamela replied. "How can I stay away when I am asked to wear this perfectly lovely green creation which you brought over?"

"You, as matron of honor, will be as lovely as the bride!" Jill exclaimed. "We'll knock their eyes out, won't we!" and she giggled with self satisfaction.

"How you worked me in as the honored attendant with such short notice, I will never know," Pamela said. "I no sooner got off the plane and you were there twisting my arm. You *know* that I cry at weddings and I truly feel that I should not threaten to ruin a perfectly joyous occasion with tears."

"Oh, you know that you won't be able to squeeze out a tear, you will be so preoccupied wondering if everything is perfect."

"Quite true. We'll survive somehow, both of us."

"And, what about me?" Ned asked. "It seems that I am the one who has every reason to be the most nervous. After all, I am assuming a tremendous responsibility in marrying someone who sees the world through rose-colored glasses." He smiled almost maternally at Jill.

"Rose-colored glasses? Why, how can you say that, Ned! I am the eternal realist, hard-nosed, with a pump for a heart instead of flesh and blood," Jill laughed.

"Perhaps when it comes to business, my darling. But, not when it comes to anything else, I am afraid. If I left it to you, you would have the whole world on our doorstep, offering shelter, food and clothing. Not that I would mind, excepting for the inevitability that I would soon run out of the wherewithal to continue sustaining them. I am only one man, you know."

"I know," Jill answered, suddenly serious. "That is precisely why I am glad that Pamela invited me over this evening." Pointedly looking into Ned's dark eyes she continued, "She called less than an hour ago."

An uneasy feeling settled over the room. Ned realized that he had been found out by the one whose innocence he thought he could always fool. It made him sorry that he had been deceiving her, and yet, he was not being false to himself when he determined that if he couldn't have one, then he would possess the other of the two unusual girls in the room. He hated his own weaknesses. Relieved, he heard Jill continue:

"However, darling, on the other hand, you are an especially good-hearted man and strong. It makes it easy to forgive and forget, especially when remembering that you would try your best to meet my expectations. Yes. You are only one man and you are becoming *my* man of your own volition in less than two days."

Their eyes hung together, naked with knowledge.

She continued to soften his discovery of her steel backbone which he had not heretofore known existed, "You are my choice as well and I love you, Ned."

"Yes, darling. Things will be all right," he rose, walked over to her and bending down, planted a kiss on the tip of her delicate nose.

Slightly coughing, Pamela suggested, "Well, now that we have all witnessed 'As the World Regurgitates,' let's get out of here and go eat dinner."

"Oooh, Pamela. The things you say!" Jill laughingly wrinkled her nose at her friend. "How appetizing."

"Where is Davie?" Ned asked. "We will wait for him. A growing boy needs a good steak every so often... or at least a hamburger with all the trimmings."

"Here he comes now. Hey Davie! Come here. We have guests who are proposing something called food. Are you interested?" Pamela sang out.

"Oh, boy. Am I interested! I could eat ten horses, fourteen goats and six chickens. I'm starved!"

Rising from the comfortable setting, they started carrying their empty glasses toward the kitchen.

"It's nice to feel at home, Pamela. I like being able to go into every little nook," Jill said.

"Do you still have the key which I gave you, Jill?" Pamela whispered. "Don't lose it and if ever you need a place to go to be alone for awhile, you just come here, as always. Play my piano, read, paint, cry, whatever, O.K.?"

They squeezed hands in agreement.

"You're the dearest friend anyone could ever have, Pamela," Jill's eyes were illuminated by her sincerity. "Thank you for inviting me over here today. I understand why you did so and appreciate it."

Pamela hugged her neck and said, "I will never forget awakening from surgery for the first time in three days and seeing your smiling face, nor hearing that cheerful, 'Hi, Pamela,' which made me realize that if I wanted to live, I must fight hard to do so." Tears popped into Pamela's eyes and she involuntarily put her arm through the arm of her friend.

"You are as dear to me as a sister ever could be." Jill brushed a tear from her own green eyes and then with a little half smile, offered a Kleenex to Pamela.

"I remember sitting in the waiting room those three days and nights. I just couldn't leave not knowing whether you would live or die. I have never had as loyal and unselfish a friend as you, Pamela. I couldn't bear to lose you. And, if lose you we all had to do, then I was going to be there when and if it happened. Davie would have needed me as much as I needed to be with him during those dark days."

"Oh, Jill. Thank you. Thank you," Pamela choked and cleared her throat. "And Jill?"

"Yes, dear heart."

"I want this marriage to be everything you have ever dreamed of. You of all people are so deserving of security and continued romance and thoughtfulness being extended to you in a marriage;" her voice became even more still as she continued, "You love him so very much."

"Thank you, Pamela. And, do you know what? If you will listen to your heart the day of the wedding, those same things can be yours also," she smiled wistfully at her friend.

"What do you mean, Jill?" Pamela questioned, looking curiously into Jill's eyes.

"You will see, you will see. Just promise me that you will not be impetuous that day. Please?"

"I don't understand, but if you must have a promise to make you relax completely in order to enjoy your day, then, O.K. You have my word."

"Are you two going to stand in the hall and whisper all evening?" Ned wanted to know. "Davie and I have taken an unanimous vote that we are ready to go to Olé's for Mexican food. May we have a second to that motion, ladies?"

Jill skipped into Ned's arms, smothering him with playful kisses.

"Yes, yes, darling. I want a cheese tortilla, a chimichanga and a cool, absolutely gigantic margarita!"

"We may as well take both cars, Jill," Ned laughingly put her from him and aimed her body toward the door. "I'll take Davie with me in the Jag and you may take his lovely mom with you in the Porsche. Good enough?"

"Great. Let's go everyone." They all piled out of the door, passing by the robin-egg blue pool which gave a tantalizing invitation for a pre-dinner swim. The gas lights were already aflame around its edges, hinting of soft desert night air and murmuring water as it moved around a lone bather.

"Oh, Mom, I forgot. I have trumpet practice at seven o'clock tonight at Joey's house. His mom is going to pick me up and bring me back. Is that all right?" Davie wrinkled up his nose against the late afternoon sun.

"Sure. Am I mistaken, or are you developing a little ambition along that line? School doesn't even start until three weeks from now. What is whetting your appetite?" Pamela asked.

"Well, if I can get my triple tonguing down pat, I stand a chance of not only being first chair, but also of being the lead horn in the school trio. Teacher said," he shyly added.

"Terrific, son!" Pamela smiled.

Ned and Jill echoed her approval.

Easing down into the Porsche, Pamela pulled her long legs in and stretched them in front of her, luxuriating in the richness of it all.

"This was quite an engagement gift, wasn't it Jill," Pamela laughed. "One thing is for sure, you won't ever have to make your last loaf of bread stretch until payday anymore as we did a year ago. Remember?"

They laughed together, enjoying Jill's good fortune. To see that she adored her fiancé was obvious and Pamela felt a sense of relief that she had acted sensibly and in good conscience to Ned's ambivalence. She intended to persuade him to become as a sibling in his feelings for her. Somehow she would persuade Ned that duty and honor were sacred.

Quietly, sad thoughts regarding Rick assailed her. She turned her head away from Jill to hide the tears and swallowed hard.

"Pamela, I was going to ask you, where is that emerald and gold hair pin which Ned gave you while you were recuperating in the hospital? Remember when he pulled two gifts from his breast pocket and handed one to you, the other to me?"

"Yes, Jill. I remember that inside your little box was also the most exquisite pearl necklace I have ever seen. And, pearls are your jewel if ever there was one. You are so ethereal and heavenly with that blond hair. They look especially angelic on you!" Pamela exclaimed.

"Oh, thank you. But, you are sidestepping the question. The pin, remember the pin?" Jill's eyes twinkled teasingly at Pamela after giving the road a look in order to cast a sideways glance at her friend.

"Oh, the pin. How I loved that marvelous emerald concoction. Well, it disappeared one day as I was riding horse with Rick," her voice caught. "I already told you."

Softly Jill interjected, "Pamela?"

Pamela sighed and looked over at Jill.

"We parted angrily from one another and I haven't seen nor heard from him since." Her face had turned more pale than usual from the painful memory. "As a matter of fact, the pin must have fallen out of my hair when I angrily spurred my horse to carry me home in my efforts to run away from him. My hair did tumble down just then." Tears blurred her vision. Camelback Road became as fuzzy as a caterpillar with yellow lines running jaggedly down its back, deformed cars going this way and that. She wiped her eyes carefully so as not to smudge her mascara.

"Do you want to talk about it?" Jill softly implored.

"I can't, not yet. But, I want to tell you. You always have such good insight into human behavior, especially where my experiences seem to be concerned. I couldn't have made it without you after Davie's father died," and her voice broke. She held her breath, trying to regain her composure. "And now for the first time since losing him, I..." she couldn't finish.

"Do you love Rick, Pamela?"

Pamela looked over at her friend who was carefully driving the car past 44th Street. The intersection was busily emptying itself, mouthful after mouthful of cars, trucks and motorcycles as if they were scurrying ants pouring from a huge orifice on a wide, black tongue.

"And life goes on," Pamela sighed wearily. "One can be dying of a broken heart and literally starving to death and yet life goes on for everyone else as if nothing is happening."

Recognizing the touch of justifiable self-pity in her friend's sensitive words, Jill's eyes filled with moisture too. "Pamela, I know that if you will give it time, you also will realize your dream."

"Do you really think so, Jill?" Pamela pathetically asked.

"Yes, I do," and Jill reached over and patted her friend's hands which were nervously twisting a wet Kleenex into even worse shape.

"Never say die!" Pamela chirped all of a sudden. Grinning through her tears, losing the valiant effort in one delayed sob, she choked and self-consciously blew her nose.

"That's what you always say, isn't it," Jill softly smiled. "You have courage."

"And you," Pamela smiled wistfully at her from across the car.

"Well, here we are. Ready for a rousing, steamy morsel which will light a fire, if not in your heart, in your mouth?" Jill asked.

Roaring to a quick stop and shoving the stick into gear after turning off the key, Jill and Pamela jumped out to join Ned and Davie who were waiting on the sidewalk in front of Olé's.

"What are you smiling so wisely about?" Ned asked Jill.

"You all will see at the wedding in a couple of days," she quietly murmured, giving Pamela a look of absolute, quiet joy.

★

After being brought home, Pamela walked slowly in the soft Arizona night past the pool which lay like turquoise in silver. Patio chairs of the same color were placed strategically at the poolside with white, round tables sporting turquoise canopies. The white fringe on the umbrellas stirred softly in the breeze as did the palm fronds which dryly whispered in a cacophony of soft rustlings. Sage from the desert a few lengths away was emitting its evening scent, and every now and then she could hear a tiny peep, as if some sleeping roadrunner was having a pleasant dream while nestling beneath the bushes which decorated the redwood fence surrounding the pool. The flames in the Roman lamps flickered warmly, giving off a soft hiss as they burned steadily in spite of the occasional gusting of the breeze.

Remembering how she used to love living in the desert where moonlit nights would find her walking alone, she looked overhead trying to see the stars which in the desert looked translucently brilliant from the dry air. She couldn't see the big dipper, nor Orion. Not even the little dipper could be distinguished because of the flow of the street and neon lights of the metropolis surrounding her. She could see the moon, however and it hung like a white disc, beautiful in its roundness.

"Just think. You are holding an American flag in your hand, Man in the Moon." Pamela smiled slightly.

Looking at the moon's loveliness reminded her of love and she felt a surge of loneliness and hurt. Unbidden, Rick's face came before her. She could see the square jaw, the violet eyes in the tanned face shaded by his sage-colored Stetson. She imagined the sparkling white of his even teeth whenever he had laughed or smiled with her. She remembered the day they had met at the lake and how her very insides had trembled, turning to liquid fire as she stood in the cool water. Thinking of it now, caused her to feel the same way and she came to a standstill, shut her eyes, and was lost in the memories of that long-awaited love for which she had been so starved.

'How could I have been so wrong? How could I have been so wrong?' She agonized within herself, depriving herself of the comfort of feeling that she was indeed lovable or even worthy of a good man's love.

'He didn't love me after all. I was just a new toy.' All of a sudden she felt so alone, so needy. Even her job had gone by the wayside when she needed it the very most for her *health* was gone. The doctor in Minnesota had been wrong. Now she remembered the surgeon telling her just the other day that for a year she would have to be a lady of leisure.

In misery she wondered, 'How does one become a lady of leisure without the dollars with which to become leisurely?' And then, 'How can I feed my son without money? Dear God, don't let my little boy go hungry... help me to become strong.'

She crossed her arms over her chest which ached with heart-wrenching anguish. Everything was gone, her husband, Rick, her health. Grasping each shoulder she slowly sank onto the edge of the pool with her feet on the top step which led into the water. Rick's face again came before her, and her anguish became the desperation of shattered love, broken dreams.

Slowly rocking back and forth as if she were a mother comforting her baby, she comforted herself. Tears poured down her ivory skin. She doubled over, placing her hands full length over her wet face as if to hide from the painful longing and disappointment with which she was being overwhelmed. She felt something trickling between her fingers, sliding wetly down her wrists to the creases of her inner elbows. The taste of bitter salt slipped between her lips. She could scarcely breathe as each exhalation tore itself upwards, twisting and wrenching against her esophagus, knifing her already tender lungs.

"Rick! Rick!" she sobbed. "What happened to us?"

Remembering his soft kisses, the firmness of his body pressed against hers; the oneness which surged between them whenever they were working together on horseback amongst the herds; the nieces and nephews and how they obviously adored him; all those things washed over her, wave after wave.

Pushing herself up from the side of the pool, one small hand swept the burnished curls from her eyes. Tucking them behind her ear on one side, she wiped her face with both hands and went to her apartment, gaining entrance through the back door which opened direclty into her bedroom. Without turning on any lights, she tossed her purse onto the chaise and laid face down on the bed.

She brought her hands to rest on each side of her head, palms down. As she nestled into the pillow, she thought that she smelled the scent of sage and leather. It was very faint, but realizing that it was a fragrance, she raised her head and delicately touched the tip of her nose against the crisp percale of the pillow slip.

'It is cologne! It is Rick's cologne!' she thought to herself, feeling as if caught in space.

'Oh, I am being ridiculous, it couldn't be! I just changed the bedding this morning and all these pillow slips smell of is the cedar which lines the linen closet.' Because of the total darkness in her room, she couldn't see anything to speak of. Bringing her shoulders back down onto the bedding, she comfortably wriggled into the soft down of the pillow. One lone tear belatedly slipped from beneath her long lashes, softly dampening her cheek.

'Oh, I just can't seem to get comfortable!' she thought, and turned her head to the left side which brought her left cheek to rest against the pillow in a slightly different spot.

"Ouch! What's that?" she raised again, rubbing her cheek. "Golly, that was cold and sharp!"

She reached for the bedside lamp. Turning it on, a soft white glow fell across the pillow, illuminating a thin strip of gold metal. Green prisms subtly played a quiet melody to her, a melody of the apparent nearness of the man for whom she longed. She felt momentarily confused, as if caught in an instant replay of something she had experienced before.

"The golden pin! My golden hair pin!" she exclaimed. Surprised she slowly gathered it in the tapered fingers and picked it up off the pillow.

'But, how could it have gotten here?' she thought.

"Rick? Rick?" she called softly, stirred by a faint hope. Apparently he had been there. Why else would the pillow retain the scent which to her was synonymous with the man? His hands must have brushed against the cloth when the pin had been placed carefully on the pillow slip. Jumping up, she ran down the adjacent hall into the living room, half expecting to see him sitting comfortably beside the fireplace. But the room was empty. The only life evident was that of the electric light which was softly shining on her Russell painting above the piano.

"Rick! Rick!" she ran to the kitchen for surely he would be there. Of course, he would be hungry!

The kitchen loomed large and cold in its open-beamed emptiness.

From the kitchen she ran to the front door, releasing the chain and bolt, pulling it open. An empty patio silently greeted her. Lighted wrought iron street lamps and cacti welcomed her with their beauty. She walked out to the spot where the cement met the sand on the driveway. Looking down, she saw the perfect imprint of a pointed boot and then another and another. Kneeling down to make sure that it was bootmarks which the silver moonlight was exposing, she felt a sand-devil bite into her knee.

"Nasty little thing," she scolded as she extracted the little stickers from tender flesh. "Thank goodness this little spiked ball of orneriness came off all in one piece!" and she tossed it away where some other bare-fleshed creature could enjoy a rude awakening.

"I should know better than to expose my skin to you," she patted the ground as if comforting an old friend. "I might love the daylights out of you, Arizona, but you sure have a bite to your kiss at times. Now, tell me, have you seen my man?" Tracing the outline of a bootprint with her fingertip, her heart beat like a trip-hammer from seeing how fresh the marks were. Getting up, she walked a few steps more, following the footprints to obvious tire tracks adjacent to the spot where the boot imprints abruptly disappeared.

"Rick!" she breathed. "Surely you have been here." She looked at the golden pin which was still tightly clasped between the fingers of her left hand. It sparkled in the moonlight. She brought it to her lips and kissed it, then held it against her heart for a long time, eyes closed, remembering the last time she had worn it; remembering the man. The pin seemed to be alive, bringing the thought that perhaps as recently as an hour earlier it had been held in the strong capable hands of the cowboy she loved.

'But, how can that be?' Fresh disappointment and a feeling of hopelessness enveloped her. 'I lost this in Rick's pasture twelve hundred miles away. He doesn't even know where in the Phoenix area I live. I purposely made sure of that by leaving only Jill's telephone number with Elsie. And, Rick doesn't even know Elsie as far as I can recall and my parents are in Europe, so there's no way it could be Rick. No way.' Sadly retracing her steps to the front door, she let herself in, securing the locks.

She leaned against the massive Spanish door and wished that Davie was not sleeping. She needed the touch of another human's care.

Chapter Ten

As it happened, after Jill and Rick had said goodbye outside her shop, Rick and Sam drove out to Rick's ranch.

"Looks like you found something with which to thrill a certain young lady," Sam guessed.

"Yes, that I have done. As a matter of fact, let's swing by her place and see if she is home. Frankly, I am hoping that she isn't there as I want to leave a little surprise on her pillow."

They turned down 40th Street heading for the address which Jill had provided Rick. Pamela's car was not in the driveway nor the garage; so Rick parked, jumped out of the car and went to ring the bell. There was no answer. He took out the key which Jill had given him, went inside and carefully shut the door behind him after checking for a security system, which he found and rapidly turned off. Then he went in search of Pamela's bedroom.

Entering the sanctity of Pamela's most private domain for the first time overwhelmed Rick with a surge of love and appreciation for all the fine things which Pamela represented to him. Her soft gentleness was evident in the selection of materials and textures, colors and objects which made her sleeping place one of relaxed elegance. The snowy, velvet bedspread, the white carpeting lent a sense of innocence and purity to his thoughts of her. Pale pinks, mauve and rich, deep browns accentuated the pristine beauty of the room. Crystal prisms gently tinkled as they hung from lights on either side of the bed. He looked around to see what was causing them to stir and noted that the cooling system was on. The air flow touched the delicate lighting fixtures, making them come alive even without being turned on.

Digging into his pocket, Rick fished out the eighteen carat golden keepsake and laid it carefully on the pillow which appeared to be on the side where Pamela would most likely sleep. He secured it slightly by making a little indentation in the surface of the pillow, realizing as he did so that the scent from his cologne would stay after he was gone, it being trapped in the percale of the pillow slip. He smiled to himself, anticipating her reaction when she would first nestle into the feathery softness, detecting his scent which she used to always relish. His heart skipped a beat and excitement traveled through his body down to the tips of his boots in spite of himself.

Hurriedly he returned to Sam in the car so as to leave before Pamela arrived home. Rick felt good inside. Now if only the State Department didn't call before Saturday, all would go as he had planned. He could attend Jill's wedding, at which time his unexpected presence would hopefully thrill Pamela. He couldn't wait to see the expression on her face when she started down the aisle and saw him standing beside Ned as his best man.

A feeling of excitement charged his adrenaline into activity again and he explained, "Life sure can be good, Sam!"

Sam looked over at him and grinned. "I'll agree with that. Here's hoping we aren't called out of town before the wedding. If they can just hold off for two or three more days. On second thought, wouldn't it be a nice surprise if when they did call, we were told that the rescue operation had already been completed?"

"That's what I am hoping for Bozo," Rick said. "It would certainly be a relief. Not that I mind helping, nor that I would back down, but one can't help but worry about Don's children were something to happen not only to my brother and his wife, but also to me. Sure, one of my other brothers or sisters would undoubtedly raise them, but most of them are older than us and have already raised their families. I think the kids would love any of the family, as would my family love them in return. It's just that when folks get older, they don't relish the same kind of activities, nor do they even see things in a youthful frame of mind which is required to raise the young now days."

"You have a point there, Rick."

Nearing the driveway of Rick's spread, they slowed to observe the view.

"This is my favorite place, Sam," Rick exclaimed. "I can't wait until I carry that little gal over the threshold through those heavy Spanish doors under that red, Spanish tile!"

"I'm rooting for you, Rick. I hope you two can get exactly what you both are yearning for. I know that sprout of hers sure is crazy about you and you'll make him a fine father, that's for sure. I wouldn't mind having that kid for my own. She's done a fine job with him."

"That she has done. She's just one fine woman!" Rick agreed wholeheartedly as he pulled the car to a complete stop at the entrance to a four car garage.

No sooner had they walked into the house when the telephone rang.

"Hello," Rick listened anxiously to whoever was on the other end of the line.

"Are you sure?" he asked. "Are they wounded?" An anxious frown creased his brow as he listened further.

"O.K. We will be ready to come the moment you give the signal. I will look for the material," Rick said. "Are you sure we will be in time if we wait that long?" After a silence, Rick agreed and carefully hung up the receiver.

"Sam?" His friend looked at Rick gravely. "We've really got a monumental problem on our hands this time."

"What's wrong?" Sam wanted to know.

"Well, the first phase of the rescue attempt has been completed. Don and Sis are safely out of the rebel stronghold, but the rainy season has set in with all its flash floods, mud slides, crumbling mountain sides, you name it, not to mention the new influx of poisonous wonders being in places where they don't usually venture. In the particular spot the rescuers and my relatives are there's been an influx of snakes, vermin and wildlife which have been pushed into the higher elevations to escape the floods which are roaring through the lowlands. Their food supply wagon has been stranded because the torrential rains washed out the bridge and the river is too swollen and swift to chance ferrying it across. Guess if they have to, they can eat grubs or make stews out of the ever present small palm nuts and potato vines. Actually they aren't potato vines, but we call them that because the leaves look exactly like a potato plant. If one puts a few hot peppers into the sauce, it doesn't taste too bad."

"Where exactly are they?" Sam asked Rick.

"Well, I'm not supposed to divulge that information until we are in our flight pattern at a certain time and place. I feel like a donkey relating that request. A more close-mouthed, trustworthy friend couldn't be had. You're tops, but they expressed the fear that someone may overhear us talking about it. So I guess I'd better keep my mouth shut."

"Understandable, and it's O.K." Sam patted his friend's shoulder acknowledging that all was taken in the right spirit. "Come on, let's go get something to eat. I'm starved!" the black-headed cowboy said as he headed for the kitchen.

★

Pamela awakened, wondering even before her eyes were open why she was so lifted in spirits. Opening her eyes dreamily, she saw something glistening on the night stand next to the alarm clock. Reaching out for it, she suddenly remembered the reason for her joy – the golden pin! Rick was around, close by. She knew that he had been standing next to her bed, that his hand had actually touched the very pillow on which her head lay. The very thought sent her into ecstasy and with a trembling hand she picked up the cherished item, bringing it to her lips to kiss that which he had held in his hands, carried in his pocket next to his heart.

Sitting up in bed, she pushed strands of hair from her eyes, stretching a little to get the kinks out. Thinking of Rick, she thought, 'Surely he will call today.' But then the thought that she hadn't even left him her unlisted telephone number made her heart sink. The old, familiar sick feeling in the pit of her stomach returned. There was no way in which he could get her number. She hadn't even had the telephone workmen put it on the center of her receivers in the house when the telephones were installed!

Trying to cheer herself, she turned her thoughts to the wedding which was to occur the very next day. She went to the closet to see the sea-green chiffon wonder which she would be wearing.

"I wonder who Ned's best man is going to be," she mused. "I really don't know any of his friends. I wonder if they are all as overwhelming as he!" With that she selected a pale lavender cotton voile blouse with matching voile skirt, coordinated lingerie with the outfit, took a wide silver belt off the belt rack, bent over to pick up matching shoes and went to the bathroom to get ready for the day. Hanging the items in the adjacent dressing room, she was surprised to hear the doorbell ring.

Hurrying down the hall while pulling on a white terry robe, she opened the door to a delivery man from Lily's Flower Shop.

"Hello, Ma'am. A delivery for Pamela Ellis."

Pamela reached out in surprise for the snow-white, oblong box which was tied with pure white ribbon into an exquisitely arranged bow.

"Thank you," she smiled as she gently shut the door. Her senses were reeling from anticipation as she opened the hall stand drawer to find scissors. As she cut into the white silky band and started to slip the bow off the rest of the way, she noticed that her hand was slightly trembling. Thoughts of Rick overpowered her and even though she knew that the flowers would be from no one else at this point in her life, she couldn't believe that they would actually be from her estranged beau.

Placing the box on her lap as she sat on the velvet coverlet in her bedroom, she carefully lifted the lid. A breath of hope and life seemed to reach out to her as she beheld the emerald green floral tissue which was carefully tucked over into a neat fold, protecting something within its depths. Hardly able to breath regularly she separated the fold and couldn't help but exclaim, "Oh, how beautiful!" as she saw twelve, creamy white, long-stemmed roses lying on a bed of deep green fern. Six barely opened buds lay on each end carefully tucked onto the bed of green, their elegant stems stretching across each other. A white card had been placed exactly in the center of the bed of stems. Pamela gingerly reached out to pick it up, fearing that Rick's name wouldn't be inside after all. Maybe Mr. Randolph and his wife had sent a welcome home gift... it would be just like them to do such a lovely and thoughtful thing. They had been known to delight her with surprises before. Carefully she opened the tiny envelope and with abated breath pulled out the card.

'Love, Rick.'

"Oh! They *are* from Rick. They are," and tears of joy popped into her eyes. A great wave of relief washed through her heart and mind. 'He does love me after all. He does, he does!' She held the card to her heart as she wept silently. 'He loved me enough to come find me and if I can't recognize someone making this kind of effort as being prompted by love, then I never will understand anything,' she reasoned to herself.

Going out to the kitchen to find an appropriate vase, she started to arrange the beautiful love gift. She was so happy, she thought she'd absolutely burst. Singing a little tune to herself, she carried the frosted crystal vase carefully to her room so as to protect the flowers from being brushed against the door as she opened it. Setting them on a mirrored organizer on her dresser, she rearranged a couple flowers, lifting one of the delicate heads to her delicate face to smell the sweet fragrance permeating from them.

'He even remembered my favorite color. Now, I *know* that it was he who placed the pin on my pillow because he noticed how I adore white.' She looked around, enjoying the subtle presence of all the colors which were embodied in the white appointments. 'It is so strange how most people think that white is an unexciting color because they think it is no color at all. Actually, it is the presence of every color we know. Guess I love it so well because of my admiration for freshly fallen snow when I was a little girl.' She started reminiscing of how excitedly she used to run to the window of her bedroom in her flannel nightie across the cold floor in order to stand in wonder as she watched diamonds twinkling and sparkling brilliantly in the morning sunshine. Not an imprint, not even any little bird tracks would have touched the newly fallen powder. How she had loved the winter wonderlands of Minnesota while growing up! 'In fact, that was my favorite season – skating, tobogganing, sleigh-riding, skiing, taking walks just in order to hear the snow squeak and crunch under my boots. Yes, I loved winter time.'

"Mom?" a sleepy voice called. "What time is it?"

Pamela walked into her son's room and knelt beside his bed. She took his little, blond head in her hands and gently roughed up his hair.

"How are you, sweetheart?" she asked, planting a kiss on his cheek which was warm from sleep.

"Oh, Mom! Kisses are for girls," he complained. But she noticed the big grin that still was spread across his face from the moment she started to tousle his already sleep-swept hair.

"You think so, do you? Well, in that case, here's *my* cheek!" and she promptly bent closer, offering her face.

Davie laughed, pulling the blankets over his head so quickly that she couldn't grab them away before he totally escaped. Laughing, she tried to pull the blankets down from the squealing, wriggling child.

"Hey, Davie. Come here, I have something to show you," she enticed.

Countering to ascertain whether or not it was truly a surprise which he would enjoy, or if it was a prelude to one of his mom's clever tricks which she pulled to get him out of bed, sleepily he asked, "Are they tickets to see the baseball game tonight?"

"No, the surprise is much better than that. Someone of whom you are very fond sent a surprise over this morning. Come on, sleepy head, come see what it is!"

"O.K. But, you have to go stand at my door or I won't take these blankets off my face. I don't want any more sissy kisses!" he pouted with half a smile and happy, twinkling eyes.

Pamela walked to the door.

"O.K., I'm standing in the doorway of your room."

Davie started to burrow out from under his cocoon, looked at his mother dubiously and gaining confidence when he saw her turn to lead him, started walking confidently to catch up with her. All of a sudden she whirled around with open arms, grabbed him midst shrieks of his pealing laughter and "Mom, no fair! No fair!" gave him a big bear hug.

"That's what you get for being such a cutie!" she laughed.

"Boy! I hope Rick hurries and finds us. I can't take much more of this!" Davie exclaimed.

"Sore head!" Pamela made a face at him and turned around to lead him to see the flowers.

As they stood looking at them, wondering aloud exactly as to when Rick would come over to the house, or call on the telephone, Davie reached a little arm around his mom's middle and laid his head against her arm.

"Mom?"

"Yes, son?"

"I was just teasing you. I really do like it when you come and give me a little kiss once in awhile. But, will you promise me something?"

"Sure, what's that?" Pamela asked.

"Will you promise never to kiss me on the cheek... in front of my friends? I'm nine, you know."

Pamela laughed and agreed.

★

The day of the wedding dawned bright and fair. It promised to be a virtual scorcher in the southern Arizona, August tradition.

"Jill, darling. Don't you want me to run down and pick up Ned's ring at the jewelers? You really don't have that much time to become utterly glorious from a nap, a good soak in bubbles and all the other things a bride likes to do in the morning of her special day."

"Thanks, Pamela, but I will enjoy the drive down to the square. I need a breath of fresh air before it becomes stifling anyway," she laughed.

"Well, is your gown pressed, etcetera, etcetera, etcetera, as the king would say in one of my favorite musicals?"

"Well, let's see. I think I would really like it the most if you'd relax and go swimming or something yourself. Why don't you give yourself a break. I want you to be utterly ravishing at that ceremony this morning. Who knows what might turn up?" Jill smiled softly.

"O.K., but neither one of us has much time in which to transform our natural shortcomings into looks of distinction. So hustle. I'll get myself ready almost to the wire and then I will wait to help you. We're donning our gowns at the church, you know. Hurry, my fair lady."

With that Pamela playfully shoved her friend out of the door.

★

"Ten on a Saturday morning never promised to be so rewarding!" Rick said with relish to Sam as they entered the cathedral vestibule.

"Can't wait to see the girl of my dreams. I really am on edge hoping those jackals don't interrupt the wedding by calling us to go early. Jeez! Once we see each other, we'll need at least a couple hours alone!"

Sam led the way down the steps into the basement of the church, asking if it wasn't unusual for a building to have a basement in that part of the country. Rick agreed that it was.

As Rick greeted Ned and started to take off his cowboy shirt, he heard a telephone ringing upstairs. Hearing it ring again, he and Sam looked at each other apprehensively.

Rick continued undressing in order to get into his morning suit of dove-grey, striped pants, grey vest, coat and tails. Carefully arranging the diamond tie pin which Ned gave him as a gift for being his best man, he heard footsteps descending the stairsteps. A knock was heard at the door. Sam went to answer.

"Telephone message for Rick Jarvis or Sam McClintock," a little, pleasant-looking woman with horn-rimmed glasses announced as she handed Sam a piece of paper.

"I am Sam McClintock. Thank you, Ma'am," and he shut the door softly upon her retreating back.

"Trouble?" Ned, who had walked in behind the lady, asked curiously.

"No, nothing important it seems," Sam drawled as he scanned the note wishing the groom would disappear for a few minutes.

Suddenly Ned hurried into the next room to find his cuff links.

Sam took the opportunity to quietly approach Rick and held the message in front of him in order that he could read it while putting the finishing touches to his hair.

"Oh, poopie!" Rick groaned. "Can we still make it to New York by four o'clock this evening if we go through the ceremony? I've just *got* to see that sweetheart of mine!"

"There are only twenty minutes left before she comes walking down that aisle upstairs," Sam drawled. "I should say you'd better be there."

"Yah! I'll make *sure* we make both appointments, by Jove!" Rick grinned.

"I'm game, boss," and his sidekick gave one last tug on his cravat.

The parish priest came rushing into the room to lend confidence to Ned's jittery nerves and to lead the men into the chapel where they stood waiting for the bride to appear at the foot of the white beribboned aisle.

★

A light, airy piece by Mozart was being played skillfully and with passion by a dark-headed violinist in the choir loft.

The deep, resonant sounds of the pipe organ which was accompanying him filled the cathedral with joy.

Stained glass windows bathed in morning sunshine, cast brilliant prisms of color onto the guests who were seated below a massive open-beamed ceiling. Mosaic colors bathed the floor, awaiting the white satin slippers of the bride and the flowing chiffon hems of her bridesmaids who quietly had appeared at the entrance to the chapel proper.

Suddenly, Rick noticed a whisper of movement at the other end of the church. He saw the girls as they appeared one by one to form a line at the entrance of the main sanctuary.

And then he saw her. All he could see were satin slippers occasionally peeping from under a matching floor-length skirt of sea-green chiffon. But, he could tell that it was her just by looking at the way in which she carried her lithe form. Never before had he seen his love in anything other than jeans, boots, swimsuit and his old shirt.

As Pamela came innocently toward the door, more and more of her was revealed. Rick's eyes traveled to her waist and as she came toward the entry the ability to see the rest of her slid on breathless anticipation for Rick. It was as if a film was being shown from feet to head and each part of her which came into view was even lovelier than he had remembered. His heavenly optics traveled from her waist, up her Grecian-swathed bodice to her lovely neck and beautiful face which was elegantly framed by a sweep of chestnut hair caught atop her head with the golden and emerald pin which he had laid on her pillow. She was carrying one white rose.

"Bozo!" Sam looked at him. "She found it!"

He and Sam smiled at the lovely vision standing with bowed head by the bride, listening intently to something Jill was whispering in her ear. He saw the one in green reach around the one in gossamer showers of white, giving a quick hug.

The music swelled into solemn strains, beautiful and moving. The bridesmaids started down the aisle, spaced evenly apart by the patient coordinator who was standing at the entrance, graciously nodding at each girl when it came time for her to start the nervous-on-the-inside, composed-on-the-outside journey to the waiting groom and groomsmen.

Rick's gaze was riveted on Pamela. Feeling the pull of someone's psyche on hers, Pamela lifted her eyes to the altar.

Suddenly her eyes met Rick's. In disbelief her mouth parted. She felt faint and it seemed as if she were sinking in delicious waves of wonder as she again beheld the beautiful violet messengers which had always conveyed his deepest feelings of love to her. She couldn't believe he was actually standing there, smiling at her. Her heart started beating wildly like the wings of a hummingbird. It seemed that no one else was in the church. There was only Rick, her beloved Rick. She wanted to run to him, run into his arms to ask forgiveness for her hasty temper. But an impatient, "Ma'am!" from the chubby coordinator jarred her back into the nuptials.

Pamela turned questioningly to look at Jill. The bride smiled mischievously, yet sweetly at her dearest friend, enjoying the surprise she and Rick had orchestrated.

Jill winked at Pamela and then motioned playfully with her slender hand that it was past time for her friend to start the long, slow walk to stand opposite the man whom she had been mourning as lost forever.

Rick watched her come down the aisle toward him.

Their eyes were locked helplessly together even as their bodies had been a few weeks after she had accepted his proposal of marriage. Suddenly, Pamela realized that she had come within a few feet of him and turn away she must. A radiant smile broke across her face as she tore her eyes away and headed for her place at the other side of the altar.

Suddenly the glorious strains of the traditional wedding march swelled over the congregation, filling the high vaulted ceiling and every nook and cranny in the cathedral with grandeur. A rustle of heavy slipper satin and illusion net told those nearest the back of the church that the bride's journey as a maiden was about to end as she proceeded down the aisle toward her life-long dream of being a wife and mother for the man she loved. A rustle of silks, linens, cottons and paper programs gently blended with the music.

Jill, her hand delicately placed atop her father's forearm, moved as if on air to her groom. As the bride left her father, Ned took her hand, tucking it securely under and over his arm. They drew nearer the priest who waited for them.

As if on cue the couple knelt, the blond beside the dark handsomeness of her groom, their hair shining in the shafts of sunlight which streamed through the windows.

Strains of the song, *Ave Maria*, carried everyone into spontaneous worship and the virginal young bride rose midst yards of satin and folds of net to walk alone to the statue of the Blessed Virgin where she knelt, enveloping the altar in a touch of heaven. Looking up at the young, benevolent face, Jill laid white gardenias and lily of the valley at her feet.

Pamela, who was watching her friend, thought that she had never seen Jill's Dresden doll beauty so ethereal, so pure.

Jill genuflected humbly, rose in a rustle of white and came back to her place beside Ned. The ceremony proceeded without incident other than the cacophony of sound which was silently shouting within Pamela and Rick's hearts as they waited to be free to speak to one another.

The recessional came skipping from the loft and Pamela felt her hand being tucked by Rick's familiar fingers into the equally familiar crook of his massive arm. She could feel every ripple of the muscle which she remembered so well. She felt as if she couldn't breathe and she had to concentrate with all of her resolve to contain the joy which his touch triggered in her being.

Finally, they were out of the door and standing in the receiving line. For a few moments they saw only each other as Rick gathered her in his arms and kissed her with relish on the lips. A small spattering of applause made them pull apart and look behind Pamela where Jill stood glowingly clapping her delicate hands as she looked impishly at Pamela.

"Aren't you happy you came to the wedding?" the bride glowed.

"Is this why you insisted I come to act as maid of honor? One can't honorably turn down one's dearest friend on the most important occasion in her life, can she! You stinker, you planned the whole thing, didn't you!" She fairly beamed from joy.

"You are right," Jill twinkled in her musical voice as Ned laughed at Pamela's excitement. Getting married and losing her was worth doing it this way and he felt cleansed inside having honored the commitment given Jill. A finer wife and lover he would never find elsewhere, he realized. Both women were good as could be.

"Thank you, oh, thank you," Pamela cried as her eyes filled with tears. Rushing to her friend, she threw her arms around white shoulders, hugging her in a momentary, tight squeeze.

"I love you, Pamela," Jill softly said. "You are the dearest sister anyone could ever have and being that I was not blessed with a natural sister, I thank Providence that He gave me one in you. A more loyal and unselfish friend one could never find."

With that, Pamela hurried back to stand beside the man she loved.

Soon everyone had gathered at the loveliest club in town for a lavish reception. It sported the usual sterling silver, traditional crystal, china and a series of swans delicately carved from ice which were set afloat in large cut-crystal bowls of punch made for the children in attendance. Guests filtered from the banquet hall through arched entries onto the patios, spilling onto the green lawns like beautifully colored butterflies. Champagne flowed from fountains, ice cream in individual shapes of Cinderella's glass slipper, was served to delighted groups of young girls. There were delicate pinwheel sandwiches of white bread inter-rolled with a delicate, pink filling which made the same little girls who 'oohed' and 'aahed' over the ice cream slippers, wrinkle up their noses in distaste over the tangy cream cheese which was the base for the pinwheel filling. Boys still in puberty had the time of their lives nipping at the champagne fountains when no one was paying attention.

"I wonder why Davie is acting so silly!" Pamela exclaimed to Rick. "Somehow this whole scene reminds me of a Norman Rockwell painting mixed with a touch of Rembrandt."

Rick laughed, "Yes, it does, doesn't it. Everyone is having such a good time. And, I think I know why Davie and his friends are feeling so great. See Jim over there? Watch him for about a minute. After he tires of teasing little Sally Matthews over her freckles, he will most probably take a sidetrip past the champagne fountain near yonder palm tree and bougainvillea."

"Rick, are you serious? Davie wouldn't do such a thing!"

"Oh, wouldn't he now? Come on, little mother, boys will be boys, especially when their mothers are busy."

"There he goes now," Pamela said in disbelief, speaking of Davie's friend who was standing behind the fountain, standing on tiptoe in order to place the straw from his soda-pop over the rim for a quick taste of bubbly.

"Why, look at that stinker and look at my son helping lift him a little higher so he can get the straw down to the champagne," she looked up with wide eyes at Rick.

"I think it is time we take that boy home for a swim and a day of horseback riding at the stables, don't you?" Rick laughed.

Pamela gazed into Rick's eyes, sparks of passion igniting unheralded. Rick's eyes looked like deep pools stirring as if they were made of the same spirits which graced the champagne fountains. Pamela touched one hand to her white forehead. Rick's nearness set her aflame and she just had to get away with him... away from all the people who were milling around unaware that another drama was unfolding before their very eyes.

As they started across the lawn to fetch her son, a waiter in white coat and black pants approached them.

"Rick Jarvis, I believe?" he inquired.

"Yes, sir?" Rick countered.

"If you will step this way, there is a telephone call for you. You may use this table, poolside, sir."

"Thank you, Mac," and Rick picked up the receiver.

As if out of nowhere, Sam appeared beside Pamela and asked if she would care to go with him over to Jill, as the bride was about to toss her traditional bouquet to the bridesmaids.

"You wouldn't want to miss this now, would you? Not with such a hot prospect as Rick turning up like a bad penny."

"Oh, Sam. You are such a rapscallion. Are you never serious?" Pamela smiled up at him.

Within minutes, Rick had found and rejoined them.

"Pamela darling, I must be leaving soon. Would you mind if we told everyone goodbye at this point? I see that Jill and Ned have escaped anyway and are probably halfway to Spain by now to visit his relatives."

"Of course, Rick," and she took Rick's arm, using the other hand to firmly grasp that of her son. She looked down at her red-faced young man, who grinned with absolute empty-headedness back at her.

"Boy! What a party!" Davie hiccuped and giggled.

"Come along, my drunken young man!" she scowled and across the lawn to the car they all went.

★

Sam drove the four of them to Pamela's house with Rick and his sweetheart sharing the back seat while Davie rode in style up front beside Sam.

"I need to tell you that I am so sorry for misunderstanding your intentions that day in the pasture. At least I feel that I didn't decipher what you were truly saying," Rick faltered.

"What did you think I was trying to say?" Pamela asked.

Rick took her hand, toying with her fingers in the way he used to during their discussions of the summer at his spread in Minnesota.

"Well, I had offered you my heart and life when I asked you to be my wife. I thought I clearly understood that you gave me an answer in the affirmative. But, all of a sudden, here was this girl whom I was supposed to marry in three weeks telling me that she wanted to go back to her career which involved a permanent move some twelve hundred miles away! To top it off, she said nothing of me joining her." He sighed.

"Rick, darling, is that what you thought I was telling you? Oh, my poor darling. I had every intention of being back for our wedding day."

Rick looked at her, tears welling in his eyes.

"Rick. Rick. How did I ever convey such thoughts into that gorgeous head of yours? I am so sorry," and she reached out to him and was enfolded in his arms which tightly held her for a few painfully sweet moments as the car proceeded toward Paradise Valley. She whispered:

"Rick, when you became angry and left before I could finish telling you everything, I thought you had lured me into your bed by proposing marriage. When you raced away from me, my heart felt as if it had been stung by a swarm of bees, the sting was so acute and painful... I thought that all you wanted was my body, and I couldn't figure out why, because after all, it's not that great, and..."

she tried to stop the flow of tears. "I thought you truly had loved me prior to that point, and," her words were drowned by his kisses as he kissed the salty wetness which was spilling onto her lips and cheeks. He tenderly kissed her closed eyes, whispering:

"I love you, Kline Traub. Oh, how I love you."

He added, "I will never cut you off short again. Never."

Pam wept in his arms, mixed feelings of joy and relief sweeping her mind as renewed faith in the man she adored filled all the hollow places of her heart.

The car pulled into Pamela's drive and soon everyone was spilling out to get changed.

"Rick, how much time are we going to be able to spend here?" Sam asked in an aside when Pamela and Davie disappeared into their individual bedrooms to change clothes.

"Well, as I have it figured, we must leave in one hour. There is a slight possibility that we may not have to go after all. Wouldn't that be a bonus, though!"

"What's happened, Doc?" Sam queried.

"Don and his wife are on the move again. Somehow, someone was able to airlift them out this morning. But, getting across the border in a light plane was too risky. So, they touched down at a mission airstrip where they are presently being hidden by the missionaries. Tonight some local men and the senior missionary are going to try to smuggle them out in barrels which are *supposed* to be filled with television equipment. Don is too big to pack anything on top of, so they are hoping that only a couple of the kegs will actually be looked into at customs."

"The danger element makes me feel sick," Sam mumbled.

"Yah, me too," Rick looked at his swarthy friend.

"But, it is that or nothing right at this point. Every entrance to the country has been virtually sealed off by armed troops. Light planes don't have a chance of crossing the border undetected. They'd get shot down either from ground fire, or from the few Migs the country has. The only feasible way to sneak them out is to place them right under the officials' noses and hope for the best." Rick looked wrung out from the turmoil going on in his soul.

"Here comes Pamela," Sam smiled, "she's still in her gown."

"Yes, and here comes her pup," Rick grinned.

"Pamela, may I take Davie for a jaunt?" Sam asked.

"Davie, would you like that?" Pamela inquired.

"Sure," he answered in typical nine year old eloquence.

"Come on, kid. Let's get out of here and leave these two lovebirds alone," and Sam and Davie went out of the door practically at a run to see who could escape the fastest.

★

For the first time since they had laid eyes on each other in a week of heartbroken silence, Pamela and Rick found themselves alone.

"Come see," Pamela whispered as Rick held her in his embrace.

Tucking her into one arm, they walked toward her bedroom. Halfway down the hall, the scent of roses enveloped them. Rick smiled quietly to himself, looking down atop the little head of the woman he loved. Suddenly Pamela felt a gentle kiss on the side of her forehead and she was turned about face, lifted up to Rick's shoulders and mouth. His arms were about her waist. She slipped her embrace around his neck and they became lost in liquid waves of love as time lost its meaning.

He carried her in six long strides to the side of her white bed, where he laid her without releasing her arms.

Gently he undressed her. Soon, they were melded together in their need for one another like the molten wax on a candle as it runs down the sturdy shaft yet to be burned. No words needed to be spoken. Their forgiveness of each other's impetuousness was complete. Their resolve to be patient in their dealings with one another was forged that day, never to be broken.

Pamela felt herself wanting more of Rick's love. But, he kept whispering that soon he would come to her, that they would become each others once more only when he could stay with her.

"What do you mean, 'when I can stay with you?'" she fearfully asked.

Rick released her to roll over onto his back. She looked over at him, her hair loose, lying in abundant waves of coppery brown across the white velvet coverlet. Her pale green dress lay about her like a frothy confection suitable for a hot summer's day, still heaped on the bed where Rick had thrown it. The emerald pin had escaped again, as if wanting to rid her of memories of Ned... as if along with Rick's reappearance in her life, things should start anew.

Thinking how beautiful she was lying in shades of green and copper upon the soft whiteness, Rick looked into the dove-grey eyes of which he had dreamed every moment since her abrupt disappearance.

"Don't be afraid, Pamela," he reached over to caress her cheek with thumb and forefinger as his hand lay gently tangled in her hair. "I need to leave again and I can't tell you where I am going nor when I will be back," he sadly said. "But when and if I return, I will come first to you and we will marry."

"What do you mean, *if* you come back?" She was alarmed.

"I can't give details; trust me, darling. Give me a few days, maybe a week or two. Until I see you again, I'll treasure the purity of your love; and I want to remember you as you look today."

She sat bolt upright in bed.

"Rick, Rick, where are you going? It sounds so ominous." She laid herself atop of him, white arms enfolding his tanned shoulders. She was afraid.

"Darling, believe me, I'll be back. You lie here bewitching me with your loveliness. What I see in you is hope for the future, new life for both of us which will hopefully commence upon the giving of new life for someone else whom I love."

"But, darling Rick. You speak in riddles," she softly objected, tracing the smile lines around his mouth with a delicate finger. He loved her touch and caught the welcome trespasser in his mouth, nipping her playfully while catching it gently between his beautiful teeth. His resumed playfulness dispelled her panic.

"Oh!" she laughed, rising from her position to embrace and kiss his mouth, her finger still caught in the delicious vice. Removing her hand from his lips to tenderly hold his face, she kissed him until they again were breathless and she again was captured beneath him like a little bird. Luxuriating in the weight of his body which was pressed against hers, they continued their conversation until she believed that, indeed, he would be back soon.

"Until I return, I want you to have this," and he reached under the pillow, drawing a small box into his hand. White velvet was placed into her palm. He closed her fingers over it, kissing them once they held the object securely. Her pale coral fingernails looked like tiny seashells against white sand and it made Rick think of tropical days and nights.

"Darling, when I return and make you my wife, would you like to become reacquainted with me on a beautiful island in Hawaii? I would love to take you to swim in its emerald waters and to lie on its white sands in the sun. You would like it so well."

"Oh, yes, yes, I would love to go with you," she exclaimed.

Kissing her, he urged her to open the box. Lying inside on yet more white velvet was an *amethyst* pin for her hair... an amethyst the color of Rick's eyes set in lace made of platinum, both caught in a heart of sturdy eighteen carat yellow gold. Seeing it for the first time made Pamela remember the first time she had ever seen Rick's golden hair only then to discover and become lost in his unusual eyes. The jewel in the pin was glowing with the same hidden lights which had caught her attention when beckoned by Rick's interest in her.

"Oh, it is gorgeous, Rick!" and she threw her arms around him in her typical enthusiastic manner. "Oh, let's coil my hair and insert the pin right away."

He laughed.

"I *wanted* to replace Ned's with something from you," she continued. "You are the man of my heart," and she carefully handed him the box asking that he dislodge the jewelry for her.

As Rick worked to remove the amethyst trinket, Pamela stood before the dressing mirror, winding her bright hair onto the top of her head. Turning to Rick she handed the older, emerald pin to him.

"Keep this with you," she whispered. "And remember every time you look at it that I love you and am praying for your safe return."

She clasped his golden head to her bosom in a sudden rush of loving feelings and kissed deeply into his fragrant curls, burying her face in the warmth of the man.

She knelt before him where he took her face between his hands and inserting the amethyst pin into her hair, kissed her over and over again, starting at the top of the chignon, down the forehead, tip of her nose, each closed eyelid and finally her tender mouth. Lifting her up, he sat her upon his knee and just held her as he had done the first night they had met... the night he listened to her sad story, comforting her with what he already had known at the time was a lasting love.

"I have won the coveted prize," he murmured, holding her close. "Now to be allowed to stay in your world is all I want," he concluded with emotion.

She nestled her tiny face into his neck.

"I will be back, my little love," he whispered in her ear, holding her close and gently kissing away traces of fresh saltiness from her trembling lips.

"And now I must go. I'm late," and he stood, lying her gently on the pillows. But she got up thinking of Davie and dressed hurriedly.

They kissed goodbye and Rick dashed away down the hall and threw open the front door to join Sam whom he heard drive into the parking lot, Davie in tow.

Chapter Eleven

Finding themselves aboard an old DC-3 which resembled something that might have gone down in Pearl Harbor, Rick reached into his knapsack for the manila envelope containing the logistics for the so-called tap dance through the jungle.

"Why hasn't anyone retired this old mama?" Sam wanted to know. "If one of us has to sneeze, we'll blow that portion of siding right off the rest of the plane!" He pointed at a section of fuselage which was haphazardly sporting wire coat hangers, sloppily twisted together in and through anything that served as an anchor between the loosened pieces of equipment.

"Look at that door hinge! One half of it's gone and the other half's goin'. Let's hope that coat hanger is stronger than she looks." Sam rubbed a weary hand through his jet black hair.

"These seats aren't exactly the best in the house," drawled Rick as he readjusted his long legs so as to relieve the threat of a charlie horse kicking him in the shins. "I think my whole trunk is falling asleep from the blood vessels being cramped on this can. What's in this thing anyway?" and Rick thumped the five gallon tin on which he was sitting.

"It looks like a five gallon can full of honey off my dad's bee farm," Sam coughed.

"Yah? Well, that ought to make for a honey of a trip," Rick concluded.

"Oh, that was bad!" Sam grimaced.

Rick gave a self-conscious laugh. "Well, none of us are perfect. That part was bad but I still have some parts worth saving, namely my little bitty hiney which is on the line at the moment."

"You'd better quit while you're ahead," Sam sighed in tired but good-natured humor. "Or at least while I'm still awake because I don't know if I can stand much more of this stuff. All of this on top of the hocus-pocus in that envelope can only mean we're in deep weeds again. It's enough to make *me* think of marriage, too!"

Rick chuckled and looked at Sam askance.

"Hey boss—" Sam was cut off mid-sentence.

"Why do you call me boss when you're an equal partner in all my ventures and you're better off than I?"

Sam laughed at Rick's outburst. "Oh, I don't know. I guess it's because you're a natural born leader and I'm a natural man of leisure. You like to work as hard as you play. And I? Well, I'd rather just play. If it wasn't for you, I'd never see daylight."

The plane rumbled heavily into the air as it groaned off the patched, clandestine runway.

Sam continued, "I guess I prefer night games, including jobs which have the cover of darkness and a bit of cloak and dagger, wrapped in intrigue."

"Then this mission must be right up your alley. I've never seen such a pitch black night in my life. Look out there. Can you see anything?" Rick wanted to know.

"You mean there's a window in this old trap?" Sam crawled off the gunny sack stuffed with something which occasionally poked through, puncturing his cammies.

Inching along on all fours, Sam suddenly was suspended in air as the plane hit a series of air currents which made it drop altitude as if it were an elevator, with the suspending rope cut.

Picking themselves up after the unexpected trip to the ceiling, Rick rubbed the top of his head.

"A lump the size of a goose egg is starting to form."

"Did it knock some sense in, do you think?" Sam laughed. "I think I cracked one of my ribs," and he ran his fingers carefully over his chest. "Come here Doc and tell me what you think."

Rick inched over to Sam. Placing his hands on Sam's body, he carefully examined him through his shirt.

"I know that I should take your shirt off, but we don't have time. I think those are the lights of the designated coastal city below us. Making sure is a bitch through this cloud cover. Hope the pilot isn't flying from memory. Think this old tub is equipped with instruments other than a stick?"

Sam peered out the tiny window. "If ya could wash the grime off this tub, ya could see something," he growled. "What's the matter, couldn't those crooks afford to scrub this flying hippo first?"

"Oh, Sam. Cheer up, the worst is yet to come and besides, my aunt once told me that the first one hundred years of life are the worst. After you get through them, 'tings start looken up!'" he finished in a Swedish brogue, bringing a smile to Sam's face which had been twisted in pain.

"Yup. It looks like you've done it to yourself, Sam. You've broken a rib all right. Here. I'll bind you up with this ace bandage I just happen to have in my magic bag," and Rick opened his medic pack. He set about wrapping Sam's chest.

The plane was settling into a landing pattern.

"You sure you'll be able to accompany me?" Rick questioned "or do you want to stay in the plane and let me jockey those barrels on board... I can do it myself, it'll just take longer, that's all."

"Nonsense! I won't be bribed into staying in this flea trap. A man needs a breath of fresh air, even if the air does smell like mildew! It's better than the graveyard feeling of this flying whale!"

Rick laughed at his friend's obvious indignation. 'Same old Sam,' he fondly thought as he closed his case, carefully tucking it back into his rucksack which he then strapped on his back.

"Can you tell me where the barrels of film equipment are to be found? Or do I have to wait until I stumble across them in the dark."

"I can tell you. But, don't let that mouse scuttling under your first class passenger seat hear you. He might tell King Rat in the jungle once we land."

They both laughed as the mouse slid across the floor while the flying whale finally beached, anxious to regurgitate its complaining Jonahs.

Someone was trying to untie the wire hangers in order to open the door from the outside. Rick busily started to unravel the wires on the inside.

Opening the door which hung crazily on one hinge, the two men found themselves peering into a set of white eyes which belonged to someone whose visage was enfolded in the darkness which hung heavily in the unbearable humid air of the Gold Coast of West Africa.

"I see you fellas put on your makeup," the stranger obviously smiled because all of a sudden Rick and Sam saw a row of glistening white teeth hanging in mid-air beneath some well spaced white eyeballs.

"Yup. Can you see us as well as we can't see you?" inquired Rick quietly.

"You got it, pal," the friendly phantom assured.

"This man just broke a rib or two," Rick said as he indicated Sam's presence verbally.

"You're not gonna let him come along, are you?" the new presence whispered.

The rat-a-tat-tat of distant gunfire grabbed their attention.

"Jeez!" the man on the ground rasped, "we've got to get out of here. Did you hear that? They are close and might find this runway. I tell ya... ya gotta leave your injured man behind."

"He insists on coming along and you needn't worry, this tough old bird won't wince. He's better half incapacitated than two men who are whole. Trust me," he said as the eyes hanging in the heavy darkness looked doubtfully at Sam's eyes which were palely staring out at him from the belly of their luxury liner. Rick jumped down.

"Come on then, follow me," the gravelly voice ordered. Suddenly, something hit Rick on the head. Stunned, he shook himself and angrily rubbed his curls.

"Hey, man. Watch the butt of that rifle of yours! That's all I need, another goose egg right next to the one I already have. My hat won't even fit anymore; and I already had to see my hairdresser for this routine in order to come home with curls for my wedding," he growled. "My bride won't even know me with black hair."

"Sorry, Captain," and Rick heard a repressed chuckle. The sore-headed man couldn't help but grin in spite of himself. "I had the gun over my shoulder and merely wheeled in an about face to show you fellows the route," a sheepish voice excused.

"Yah? Well, no mind – but do your wheeling on the parade field, not in this black hole. Carry on." Rick reached stealthily into the belly of the whale, after turning around to feel for Sam's presence in case the injured party proved unable to go along during the jump from the plane.

"No help needed, I see," whispered Rick. "You're out already."

"Right, boss," Sam's teeth appeared in a wide row through the darkness belying the sharp spasms of breath that overtook him momentarily as he adjusted to the broken ribs. "Let's go. I'm as ready as I'll ever be."

As the three men scrambled for cover in the brush which lined the airstrip, Sam whispered, "Why in the world do we have to sneak around in a country which is an ally to the free world?"

"Well," Rick panted back, "one never knows who is a citizen and who isn't. It's the ones who aren't we're concerned about, not the ones who are. And, since we aren't familiar with the area, we need to act accordingly. All we know at present is that the barrels of film and equipment were smuggled through the borders, false bottoms undetected. All the contents are safely hidden here (and he stressed all)... but for how long they will be safe is anyone's guess. The contents are a wealth of information as to the coup."

The three men had been struggling hotly through twelve-foot grass and brush.

Rick continued, "I doubt that safe passage for any of the contents is guaranteed until the barrels land in the U.S. – if then."

"Hey, you fellas," the new guide whispered. "For being so smart, aren't you being a little dumb whispering so much? You'll wake the dead!" he scolded.

"For a young kid, you sure have a lot of lip," Rick couldn't help but smile at the honest face which had started taking shape as his eyes gradually became adjusted to the darkness.

"No offense, please," the young man said as he stopped short and started unraveling a cord from his belt loop. "It's just that I expect you to know that whispers can bring bad luck around here. Come on, tie this nylon cord from your waist to Sam's and let's get the H out of here." He eyed the sudden density of brush and trees.

"Seems to me that this will get all tangled up in foliage," Sam muttered, trying to see the tops of the towering timber above his head.

"If you get tangled, you can be cut free by one of us and follow the trodden grass back to the plane. Being tied together is better than getting lost in the jungle on a moonless night like tonight," Rick reasoned. "Once in here you won't be able to see anything."

It seemed as if they crawled on their bellies for half the night. Occasional taps of gunfire in the distance kept them from complaining about sore elbows and assorted pokes from underbrush.

"Yipes! Damn! Drivers-O!" their guide exclaimed as the rope took a lurch upwards and began dancing around.

"What's going on?" Rick edged closer, muscles tensing making ready to do or die.

"On your feet, guys! Jump over this freeway of driver-ants before they make Swiss cheese of you," the young man brushed frantically with his hat, swatting cammies, arms, legs, feet in a real tap dance.

Rick quickly unearthed a vial of kerosene from his front pocket. "I shouldn't be using this stuff, the scent will attract the wrong people if they're in the vicinity, but dammit! We need you to help us find Don and Sis." Rapidly pouring half the contents into his blackened palm, he recapped the tiny tube with his teeth while rubbing his hands together. In one swoosh of movement, his new friend was covered from head to toe in fumes fit for a room full of bed bugs.

The sting was incredible to the hapless young fellow. He didn't know which was worse, the fire from the carnivorous insect bites or the remedial stench and bite of the yellow liquid. "Just don't light any matches, you Bozos!" he adjured. "Thank God none got up my pants. Never have I appreciated these boots in the tropics before...I'll never complain again!"

"You O.K., fella?" Rick compassionately asked.

"Yes, sir!"

"Then carry on. Your clever attempt to get out of this holiday safari won't work with me," Rick chuckled and patted the kid on the shoulder. "We all have our itty-bitty's on the line and times-a-wastin."

"Gottcha," and Rick was saluted good naturedly.

Finally the three emerged onto a little footpath which led to the edge of a river. Scrambling to a canoe which was covered with fronds of palm trees, the men picked it up and crouched low across the sand to the suddenly deep river which was flowing through the twisted roots of tall hardwood trees.

"Don't I recall having seen crocodiles in places like this?" Sam wanted to know.

"Well, if you did, don't think about it now unless you happen to see one. Then, save yourself or whoever needs saving and run like hell!" Rick advised.

"Gee, thanks," Sam exhaled laboriously, lifting the canoe high overhead to clear a grey root which twisted out of the murky water to a height above his own six foot two inch body. Straining for all he was worth against the sharp pain which cut into his chest like a knife, Sam eased the tip of the vessel onto the surface of the water. He was soaked with sweat and algae from the still water at the river's edge, as were his pals.

Rick heard Sam catch his breath and worried, but had enough respect for Sam's courage and ego to keep from questioning him. He knew that if Sam reached the end of his endurance, Sam would be the first to let them know so as not to impede progress. All three of them automatically knew how to get along in strange surroundings and he knew that Sam was memorizing every detail through which he passed in case he became separated from the other two. His broken ribs, or some unforeseen happenstance could easily wean him from the little group. But, Rick knew that Sam's determination had always outmatched most and felt confident that he would be a part of the threesome until they brought their precious cargo back to the flying monster.

Stepping atop a slimy trunk, Rick started climbing into the canoe. Reaching for a thick vine which stretched from the tree top as it swayed back and forth in the waters below, he gasped, "God Almighty!" as the vine whipped into life in his grasp. "A *black snake!*"

Vicious strength almost matching his own entwined him as he felt himself falling. They slammed violently into the water, sinking like rocks. His hands slipped up to grab behind the strong head of the viper which struggled against Rick's strength in an effort to sink fangs. Whiplashing with the head, he freed his left arm, searching for his knife. Up they came. River weeds reached up to devour his feet, already heavy in combat boots. Tepid water charged into every hole in his head as the struggle torpedoed them again. His lungs started to burn, longing to take a breath as the river closed in over his head.

"Damn! I'm not finished! I refuse to die, drowned like a rat!" Exhausted, he forced his legs to slow down, disentangling them from the growth beneath his struggle. With a mighty kick, he forced his slimy foe and self towards the surface where he gasped long and deeply to fill his lungs before the fighting monster plunged them back beneath the water.

"Take that, you low-life!" and his left hand rapidly slit the pulsating mass beneath his right hand. Over and over and over again he stabbed and slit until the incessant writhing started to resemble a gentle, compulsive jerk.

Rising to the top, water poured from his hair, cascading down his forehead into his eyes forcing them shut. With a shake of his magnificent head he blew water out of his stinging nose, throwing the remains of the twelve foot black snake from him in disgust. The tail seemed to die last as it re-wrapped itself around Rick's left ankle.

"What the hell..." and he angrily tore the dead flesh from him.

Treading water strongly against the current, the suddenly tired man peered into the darkness in search of the canoe... "Nothing. Nothing. Chrissakes – it's so dark out here." The river sloshed wetly over, in and around obstacles along the bank, sounding like old-fashioned buttermilk clogged with chunks of butter being poured into a pig trough.

Suddenly, as the moon scuttled briefly from behind the clouds, a glimmer of pale light caught his eye. And attached to that tiny shaft of cool brilliance was the canoe.

'Hallelujah! There's the guys! Hot damn! Thought I was going to die and be the second one to leave Pam, didn't ya,' and he made a face to match his raised fist, squaring them both in the direction of the recent battle.

Making a mental note of the canoe's location, he swam quietly, strongly in a straight line as the moon gently receded behind the shrouded heavens.

'Hey, Moon – come out one more time. I need to see that faint light again.'

As if beckoned by a force stronger than circumstances, the clouds parted into wisps of gossamer sometimes hiding the moon, sometimes revealing her. And against the silver with which she bathed the river, Rick was able to see that eerie glimmer of pale light atop the emerging silhouette of the canoe. Careful not to ripple the river's surface, nor to splash, Rick hurriedly approached his friends who were quietly poking long poles into the water hoping to find him.

"Pst! Pst! Over here – I'm over here," Rick loudly whispered, still following the pale pinpoint of light.

"Hot damn!" Sam grinned... "We thought we lost ya this time, boss." He reached down, pulling Rick onto a big tree root.

"Yah? Well, you almost did, Bozo. God, I'm tired!" and Rick lay panting for breath, face down.

"Climb in here and get off that tree before you meet another jungle pal, you sorry son of a bitch. Jeez! Am I glad to see you!" and Sam steadied the canoe while Rick clambered over the bow reaching for the homing light.

"Look, pal. I might be glad to see you, but I'm not *that* glad. What are you fumbling on my chest for? Are you daft? I'm not Pamela!" Sam backed away.

"Hold still, you clown. I just want to see what that light is that is glowing on your shirt! That's what brought me back to the boat. What in the hell is it?"

"Oh. This?"

"Yes, that," Rick said as his fingers closed around a familiar, delicate object. Prolonged silence; and then, "I don't believe it. I just don't believe it... the golden pin. Pamela's golden pin. I thought this was fastened inside my cammie pocket." Turning his face upward to see Sam more clearly, "You a thief or what?"

"Heck no. Keep your frickin shirt on. Your temper is flaring just like it did the day you found this pin in the grass of the pasture back home." Sam threw Rick's hand off his chest. "Now listen!"

"This better be good. That thing is the most precious object in my possession." With bowed head Rick added, "And, it just saved my skinny behinder from never making its owner my bride..."

Silence ensued briefly. "Actually, if it hadn't been on your shirt, my future would have been looking pretty dim right now."

The three men paddled silently down the blackened waterway, the moon having long since vanished once more.

Sam quietly answered Rick's question, "When you took a dive with that vine, something came bouncing into the canoe... you almost tipped us over, there was so much thrashing around. We thought sure we'd be detected; but the water carried you away and we held fast to the tree roots hoping that you'd eventually be able to find your way back to the same place you'd left us. Anyway, like I said, something hit my boot. Thinking it was a scorpion or some cousin of a creepy crawler, I used my penlight to see what had hit me. There was that pin you're so fond of. So, I pinned it on my shirt so's not to lose it until I could see to put it in a safe place like my rucksack."

"He was going to give it back to you, sir," the ghost-like figure at the head of the canoe whispered. "Quiet, you two!" He stopped his paddle from surfacing for the next stroke.

Something heavy landed on a branch on shore making it snap. Rustling leaves made the men freeze, crouched low in the vessel. The canoe drifted purposely, silently along, caught in the flow of the river.

Whatever it was that had made the noise slipped into the water. Nervously looking behind him, the young guide caught sight of a penlight being used half a mile to the rear.

"Hang on," he whispered, turning the canoe sharply to the left. "Now, paddle as if your life depends on it because it does. There's a boat full of hostile hombres bearing down on us."

And they poured steam into dodging this way and that, in and around gnarled roots, pockets of swamp grass and leaves. Finally breaking into clear water, the men wound their way rapidly up a tributary which had been hidden by jungle growth.

About a mile upstream, the canoe was guided to a makeshift dock. They again scrambled to get out, two men portaging the canoe while a third dusted the ground behind them with a palm frond to cover their tracks before leaving the imprint of scattered monkey feet.

"Some rabbit foot you have there, friend," Rick observed after they had reached the safety of the bush.

"Yah, it may look gory but it comes in handy at times like this."

A thatched hut was pointed out to Rick and Sam.

"Follow me," the young guide said in a voice so low Rick wondered if he had really heard him say it. They ran to the building.

They quietly slid one by one through the open doorway, where suddenly Rick found himself face to face with his brother whom he hadn't been able to get out of his mind during the past, uncertain months since working together over Pamela's shattered body.

The twins embraced, so overcome by emotion that they couldn't utter a word. Breaking apart, they hurriedly followed the guide and Sam who motioned them on.

"Where's Sis?" Rick mouthed silently to his brother.

Don held a finger against his lips and pointed to the darkness ahead of them. Rick nodded and followed.

They walked swiftly through a space in the mud wall which brought them into a larger room. A fire was burning at the other end in an earthen fireplace made without sides or chimney, but formed out of clay into a four by six-foot working area. Smoke was rising to a hole in the center of the thatched roof, a black pot was sitting on grey-white coals which to an inexperienced eye would appear to be cold and dead. Rick knew that they would be scorching hot, more so than those which were glowing brilliantly around the edges of the flaming wood in the center of the fire.

Over against the mildewed wall of whitewashed clay, lay a figure, pathetically thin. Even though the person's face and limbs had been charcoaled, Rick recognized his sister-in-law. Hurrying to her side, he squatted down, shimmying out of his rucksack to get at his med kit. Listening to her vital signs, he noted that her blood pressure was not good, nor was her pulse strong.

"What happened?" he asked his brother.

"She's been suffering an acute attack of Black Water Fever. I don't know how she has survived, but she is starting to mend. One thing is for sure, I can't let her be stuffed back into a barrel again. It will kill her this time. She almost didn't survive it two days ago. We are going to have to carry her on a gurney to the plane. Screw the barrels!"

"Of course," Rick agreed. "Once to the canoe we can lay her in the bottom where she can't be seen. Since we're taking her out in plain view, would you like to try it cold turkey, too?"

"I'm game for anything. I think I can be of greater assistance if I'm free to tend her needs. If I am not in a barrel and taking care of her, that will leave you free to handle the defense if any is needed."

"O.K.," Rick said, "Let's get this mama back to her four babies. Let's go, we have only a few hours of darkness left to get back to the plane."

They lifted the unconscious woman from the pallet onto a makeshift gurney of bamboo poles and thatch. Rick and Don decided to carry her, being that Sam had enough to do in getting his own injured self through the difficulties lying ahead.

Suddenly, excited, angry voices were heard.

Jumping into action, their young leader shoved Sam toward yet another door, face down onto the floor. Peering out of an opening in the side of the hut, he exclaimed, "Just what I thought! We've got to get out of here *now*," and lifting the pot off the fireplace, motioned to the black man and woman who owned the hut to help him.

In amazement, Sam and Rick watched as the three hurrying figures lifted what proved to be a false floor, raising the entire bed of burning coals and crackling fire onto hooks which the man of the house had hastened to pull from the rafters overhead. A trap door which had been hidden directly under the pot was lifted. Big enough to accommodate two people walking side by side, Rick and his brother had no trouble carrying the gurney through. Instead of finding steps, they encountered a gradual incline to descend as if made especially for the evacuation of wounded and ill persons.

"Run!" Sam urged as he followed at the rear, pulling the trapdoor quietly in place above his head. Loud voices could be heard directly outside the hut, shouting abusive language.

"God help that poor man and his wife if they get caught lowering the fireplace," Sam murmured.

A soft thud was heard overhead as the grated fireplace landed the last six inches onto the platform more hurriedly than usual. The scrape of iron against iron was heard indicating to the fleeing party that the cast iron pot had been rehung. They could hear something scraping and scraping.

"What's that?" Sam anxiously called through the gloom to the guide's back as they ran behind the jostling gurney borne between the two brothers at a trot. The floor of the tunnel turned uphill.

"Nothing to worry about. The man's wife is already stirring the palm butter and thank God, we're not in it!"

"Thank God and Greyhound, we're *gone*!" Sam rejoined.

Angry shouts flared up again, but were indistinguishable because of the distance which had grown between them and the hut.

Finally, they broke into a clearing. The river lay before them, winding like a snake into the blackness of night. They had completely skirted the tributary which had guided them to the hut.

"Where are we, pal?" a panting Rick asked the young guide as he wiped his brow with a sweat-soaked sleeve.

"We're approximately half a mile from the entrance of the tributary which we took to get to the hut. Here, help me free this thing," and so ordering, he bent down hastily to remove a termite hill from its obviously secure mooring.

"Good God! How can you lift that thing so easily?" Rick gasped.

"Easy. How do you like my six foot papier mâché wonder? I'm an art major, or was. This was easy to devise. Well, don't just stand there with your mouth hanging open. Help me get this raft into the water!"

Buried in the earth beneath the fourteen foot round base of the termite hill was a raft, securely built, complete with poles and tin barrels full of food and water strapped to the round poles of which it was made.

"Where are the barrels of T.V. stuff?" Sam asked as the four men panted, tugging the raft from its hiding place into position on their shoulders.

"They are already on the way to the U.S. aboard a freighter, thanks to the local government. They have helped with this entire rescue operation and we have them to thank that we are safe so far. But if we don't cut the jabber, we may not be safe much longer. Let's get that woman safely secured onto this raft and boogie."

Rick and Sam ran to pick up the gurney which had been laid carefully in a dry spot, easily attendable if the need arose while the raft was being taken to the water. As the men loaded the sick mother, their guide restored the termite hill, brushing and patting the earth carefully around the base so as to make an undisturbed, totally natural, weather-beaten appearance. Cutting a rope hidden in the thick foliage overhead, a prearranged jungle consisting of brush, palm trees and natural effects fell around the termite hill. The whole chore took him less than five minutes.

Running to the banks of the river, he leaped aboard and started poling the raft out to the swift current.

Shots were heard in the distance; their youthful guide bowed his head and with an angry gesture, wiped moisture from his eyes. The movement didn't escape Rick's keen eyes.

"I'm sorry, man," he comforted quietly, as he sadly remembered the couple in the hut.

"Their lives apparently weren't worth a pinch of snuff to those bastards," the young fellow ducked his head to hide suddenly wetter eyes. "Come on, let's get the hell out of here. With a little luck, we've got smooth sailing ahead for about four miles, then we'll pull ashore, bury this little gem in similar fashion as how we found it and walk the last half mile to the plane. It shouldn't take us over another hour and a half."

"That so?" Rick inquired.

"Then, we'll be on our way to Paris, a change in transportation and homeward bound," the glum, barely-a-man informed. "We're supposed to get to New York by tomorrow evening," he growled. In spite of his inner pain, the thought of home made a tremulous smile appear on his face, easing the sorrow he felt over the couple's obvious sad end.

"Did you see that?" Rick whispered to the kid as the raft floated rapidly along.

"You mean the lights which occasionally flicker on the shore?"

"Yes. I've noticed them for some time now. It seems that they are evenly spaced and as we pass, a signal is being given."

Rick, Sam and the other unlikely soldier of fortune looked at each other and then over at their precious human cargo. The moon kept threatening to expose itself.

"We're sunk if the clouds roll away before we get to the graceful whale," Rick surmised.

"Yah, those lights along the shore aren't signals from friendly hombres," the youngster said. "Hear those drums? The language they're transmitting is peculiar to this part of the country. I dare say that they aren't of this area at all. If they were, I'd be able to decipher the messages."

Even Don joined the others in looking at their guide, taking new notice of the amiable stranger.

"How?" Sam wanted to know.

"I was raised on a mission where my folks were missionaries. As a matter of fact, I was born in a thatched, mud hut similar to the one you saw tonight. The mission hospital wasn't ready yet and neither was the parsonage. So, Mom gave birth in our makeshift home."

"Then you've grown up here," Rick quietly assumed.

"Yes, that's true. For that reason I opted for this assignment when I heard about it. I know every path and village around this area, not to mention the people. The natives around here are what our relatives in the midwest would call good folks."

"Did you know the man and woman who helped us tonight other than as contacts?"

"Yes, I used to play with their kids while we were growing up and then went to college in the States with their son."

"Speaking of them, who devised that ingenious fireplace?" Sam asked.

"Yours truly," the young man smiled. "I also thought it'd be better to make a ramp instead of steps once inside the tunnel because the purpose of the whole project was to help escapees if need be. I figured that most who get caught in any type of conflict end up being wounded, so thought that'd be ideal for gurney-bearing; in fact, all types of evacuation."

"It sure proved to be a good conclusion on your part tonight, pal," Rick said appreciatively.

"Barrels roll down it well, too," the boy said modestly.

"Yeow! Watch out!" Rick ducked as a barrage of gunfire broke the quiet of night, pinging bullets into the water surrounding the raft. Small explosions of water shot into the air like miniature Old Faithfuls.

"Stay low and head for that glow in the sky." Everyone looked to see what their guide was pointing out. The raft groaned under its heavy load of bodies as they swung it around midst the confusion of incoming gunfire and swirling current.

"Ugh!" Don's frame bent double.

"Dammit, are you hurt?" Rick crawled toward him, water seeping into his shirt armpits and jeans as a whirlpool caught the clumsy raft broadside.

"Just winged. Man your pole, we can tend to me later."

"Hang on you fools," Rick ordered and the crew headed for sheltering shadows under trees which lined an overhanging cliff. The barrage of fire grew heavier as they pulled closer to land. Shadowy figures scurried under the trees overhead.

All of a sudden, the rocky wall of the cliff stared them in the face a few feet away.

"My God! We're gonna hit that damn thing!" Sam exclaimed as he jumped over to the gurney on which the helpless woman lay. Her wounded husband edged closer to her also, babying his left shoulder, blood seeping through the fingers of his right hand. Deftly loosening the bands which held the gurney and raft, Sam lifted the unconscious woman into his arms.

Rick's brother braced himself for impact, but to everyone's utter amazement, the wall moved, opening wide to let the raft and its hapless crew inside a lighted waterway.

Green slime and lizards covered the walls of the fetid refuge, but the sudden cessation of bullets seemed heavenly and Don decided that he'd rather be where he was – the pox on the lizards.

"Stay right here. I'll be back in a jiff," the blond art major wound a rope around a peg in the cavern wall, jumped off the raft onto a slender piece of rock and disappeared into the depths of the cave. After a few minutes he came back.

"Let's get this thing carried over a few yards and we'll tie her up. We can't bury the raft as I had intended because the river bank is swarming with hostile foreigners. But, we're safe enough here and can leave the raft without it being detected."

"Let's go," Rick jumped off the raft, followed by Don and Sam who had laid the sick woman back where she'd been lying.

The four men carefully lifted the raft out of the water, lizards scurried underfoot.

"Here we go, set it down," Blondie ordered indicating a hiding place behind a steep incline on the cave floor.

Untying and lifting the gurney off the craft, the men took turns carrying Sis until they had to stop to rest.

"Where in the hell are we?" Sam demanded. "All it seems we ever do is run through tunnels and squish the daylights out of lizards underfoot."

"Well, you're still free and alive, aren't you, pal? Where do you think you are, at Maxims?" the young man smiled. "Look up there, Smiley. See that trap door?"

They all peered through the gloom upward.

"Wait here and be quiet," he continued. Reaching above his head, he gave a jump in order to grab a rope which was tied horizontally so as not to be seen from below. The rope's end came down with him and he gave a gentle tug. Slowly the trap door swung toward them and his three astonished partners found themselves staring into the fuselage of the grey whale.

Steps lined the trap door. Checking Sis's protective bindings, they hastened to ascend, bearing their precious cargo with them. Once inside the plane, their interesting companion grabbed a bamboo pole which was leaning against the wall and stretched it into the hole from which they had just climbed. A hook on the end of the device slid into a ring on the trapdoor and it was pulled silently back into place. Drawing the pole back into the aircraft, he then shut the trap door in the belly of the fuselage, secured it, wiped his brow and gave three sharp taps on the partition toward the enclosed cockpit.

The lumbering haven of near safety came to life and started to roll heavily to position at the end of the runway, lights still off. Suddenly they took off, the plane gaining momentum like a hippo charging from the shallows of some African stream. Air currents lifted the heavy wings and oversized belly of the contraption, wheels reluctantly lifted into their berths to be tucked safely away until needed for landing.

Looking out of the window, the passengers could see red and yellow flashes of light popping everywhere from the edges of the airstrip.

"Looks like we had a farewell committee. They're giving us a regular Fourth of July send off. Look at those fireworks!" Sam exclaimed.

"Thank God we're out of range, providing no one has a stinger," Rick sighed as he tore his brother's shirt open to examine the gunshot wound. Deftly cleaning the evacuated hole and bandaging it tightly, he patted his brother's black curls. "You'll heal up in no time, Poncho. Now to check Sis out and then if you all don't mind, I'm going to crash."

Rick wearily inserted stethoscope receivers into his ears, carefully placing the end through Sis' buttonholed shirt, checking several points until satisfied. After a thorough examination of vital signs, he tucked a wadded-up cammi under her head.

"Now," he sighed, nestling against a couple of stuffed duffle bags, "wake me up when we get to Paris and don't let me miss that flight home! I've got a little gal to go see and a preacher to employ." So saying, he reached inside his pocket and screwed something loose from its depths. Holding the screw in one hand and pulling out something else with his other, a soft, throbbing glow sparked in the dim cabin light. A cool glint of green caught Sam's eye and with a disbelieving glance at Rick, he said:

"The golden pin! You nuts or what." He scratched his head, continuing... "When I gave it back to you in the river, I figured I'd never see it again. Thought it'd get jostled out of your pocket again, the way you grab hold of 'vines' and such. By the way, Bozo, why'd you grab a vine in the first place? You know better than that!"

Rick grinned, "Aw heck. If anyone ever wrote a book about this kind of nonsense, you'd have to fight a snake somewhere along the line. Capice? Savvy?"

"Yah and I savvy something else. That pin of Pam's. A good luck piece if ever I saw one. Without it the river would have done you in even though the 'vine' was wasted."

"What worked for me was the *love* this little trinket symbolizes, I dare say," Rick softly assented. "She doesn't know where I am, but I bet she's got us on her mind, holding us up to our Maker constantly. Positive thinking and faith are winners when tripled with love," and Rick fastened the golden pin onto his shirt and fell fast asleep.

★

"Oh, Sweet Pea! How good it is to have you in my arms once more." Rick rolled over in the white silk sheets, drawing Pamela on top of him. Her breasts crushed softly against his hard chest.

"Are you happy, Mrs. Jarvis?" Rick whispered in her ear. "Were the nuptials to your liking?"

A blush from joy and lovemaking had set Pamela's exquisite face aglow. Her eyes said it all as they beamed in utter fascination; limpid pools of grey melted by love as she gazed upon her husband of exactly six hours.

"I love you so much – even if your hair *is* black until the dye washes out," she sweetly said, as she lay her head on his bare shoulder, kissing the hollow of his neck. Her burnished curls were spread across his chest; the veil and silk charmeuse wedding gown shimmered, barely orchid, on the white carpet beside the bed. Next to them lay something old and something new... both called the golden pin.